Petits Canapés

A Guide on Making Luxurious Finger Foods

Dominique Heitz

Ukiyoto Publishing

All global publishing rights are held by
Ukiyoto Publishing

Published in 2021

Content Copyright © **Dominique Heitz**

ISBN 9789362697967

All rights reserved.
No portion of this publication may be reproduced, stored in any electronic system, transmitted in any form or by any means, electronic, mechanical, photocopy, recording, or otherwise, without written permission from the author.

Events, locales, and conversations have been recreated from memories. In some instances, in order to maintain anonymity, names of individuals and places have been changed. Some identifying characteristics and details such as physical properties, occupations, and places of residence have been changed. The names, places, and/or people are fictitious. Any that seem real is created from the imagination of the author.
The names of cities, towns, and characters are also a fictitious form of writing.

This book is sold subject to the condition that it shall not by way of trade or otherwise, be lent, resold, hired out or otherwise circulated, without the publisher's prior consent, in any form of binding or cover other than that in which it is published.

www.ukiyoto.com

CONTENT
BY TYPE

VEGETABLE

Asparagus and Mushroom	14
Baby spinach flan and ratatouille	17
Baby veg garden in a glass	20
Beetroot and Goats Curd Marshmallow	23
Curried Cauliflower, Truffle and Zucchini Rolls	26
Fried Crumbed Camembert	30
Macadamia Duxelle tartlet	33
Pickled Cucumber and goats curd	36
Porcini, kale and pine-nuts spring rolls	39
Potato and truffle croquette	42
Tomato and Strawberry Gazpacho	46
Thyme, feta and onion mini quiches	48
Watermelon and Mozzarella skewers	52

FISH, SEAFOOD

Coffee curd Kingfish and cranberry	56
Crab and Prawn Tortellini	60
Crispy Prawn	64
Cured Ocean Trout and Avocado	67
Moreton Bay Bug wrapped in betel leaf	71
Oyster with Champagne and Coconut Foam	74
Pan fried Scallop, pear and black garlic	76
Potato fritter and anchovies	80
Smoked salmon and Herb Waffle	83
Tuna, avocado and salmon caviar	86

CONTENT
BY TYPE

MEAT

Chicken Roulade and Jerusalem Artichoke puree	90
Chorizo arancini, Piquillo sauce	94
Duck and Peach skewers	98
Lamb Chop with chimichurri	102
Mini Peri Peri Chicken Burger	104
Pork and Pistachio Rillettes	107
Puffed Lamb with Pea puree	110
Sirloin Beef on Prawn Crackers	114
Wagyu and Mandarins Cigars	118

SWEET

Brownie Skewers	122
Chocolate Ganache spoons	125
Eaton Mess in a glass	128
Ice Cream sandwich	132
Mascarpone in a Glass	135
Mini Basil madeleines	137

CONTENT
BY RECIPE

Duxelles	14
Flan	17
Ratatouille	17
Hummus	20
Marshmallow	23
Curried cauliflower	26
Crumbed Cheese	30
Cranberry salsa	30
Pickling liquid	30
Porcini spring roll	39
Potato croquette	43
Gazpacho	47
Quiches	48
Caramelized Onion	48
Salsa Verde	52
Fish Curing mix	57
Cranberry Gel	57
Tortellini	61
Brown butter sauce	61
Crispy Prawn	65
Sauce Chilli	65
Avocado Cream	68
Puffed Rice	68
Sauce Ginger	71
Foam Champagne	75
Pear and soy dressing	77
Black garlic puree	77
Fritter mix	81
Waffle mix	83
Tuna tartare	87
Artichoke puree	91
Chicken roulade	91
Arancini	95
Piquillo sauce	95
Chimichurri	99
Lamb Chop	103
Peri Peri	105
Aioli	105
Pork Rillette	107
Puffed Lamb	111
Pea puree	111
Prawn Crackers	115
Sirloin Beef	115
Skid sauce	115
Sauce yogurt	119
Wagyu cigar	119
Brownie	123
Chocolate ganache	126
Meringue	129
Elderflower jelly	129
Sponge	132
Madeleine	136
Tiramisu Cream	137
Coffee Jelly	137
Chef's tips	**10**
Receipes sourcing	**140**
Copyright	**141**
One more thing	**142**

PREFACE

What is Finger Food?
Canapes, dim sum, tapas, mezze, antipasto, izakaya, or simply snacks…
There are so manydifferent names, for so many countries or cultures.
They have all one thing in common: they areall finger foods.

This book is actually in itself, much like a Finger Food
Small recipes, a few food-items put together, for you to try out, in one bite! With my many years as a Chef, I cooked a lot of finger foods, some great, some average, it is always a challenge to share recipes with people with different cultures or backgrounds. Everybody has his own taste and preferences, their own cultural food habits or even dietary requirements. But I always find great joy in bringing food, new recipes or tailored dishes to people willing to taste, even if they end up not liking it,
but at least they tried.

*"Making food for other people to like,
is first to love this food yourself!"*

That would be the daily challenge of any Chef, anybody who is cooking for other people. Often people try to over complicate, make it too fancy and lose yourself in fusion or modern approaches. If you want to share food, share food that you like.

Over time I realized that sharing food was something special, something people love to do. Of course it is always different, depending on which side of the planet you live. But sharing food is always a good feeling, passing the platter to someday, showing respect or just making sure your loved ones are fed. It always comes from a happy place, it always comes from the heart.

When I thought about the next book I like to share,
I decided to select a few items to share, easy to make, that would be nice and achievable in your own kitchen. In this book I did split all recipes into three different categories, to be easy to find at any time.

So go and try, organize parties, invite your friends and family and show them that you can have a great time together, even if you have to do it with social distancing and face masks. Food has always been a moment of gathering and sharing, and we have to make sure it stays that way.

BACKGROUND

I am a French chef, born, raised and trained in the North-East region of France: Alsace. Close to the German border, I grew up in a tiny village, enriched by the mixed cultures of both countries.

When I started learning about becoming a chef, I had no idea that it would get me to so many different countries and cultures, especially in Australia on the other side of the planet. I will always remember one of my English teachers back in High school. We had to choose a career path for our future and to also pick the college or apprenticeship course. I had 2 things I liked the most, my joy for computers, video games and my joy for cooking and baking. My English teacher's answer was straightforward and to the point "your English is not very good, you should not pick any career involving English language!"

Thanks for proving me wrong...

After 20 years' experience in kitchens all around the world, I always loved sharing stories and recipes. I find that food always holds a lot of history and culture that enriches our lives and creativity in the food we create. Most importantly food carries emotions and triggers our memories…

"GOOD FOOD IS THE FOUNDATION OF GENUINE HAPPINESS"

I will always remember the first time I stepped into a professional kitchen, on my first day on the first hour, even before I was holding my chef knife! The Head chef and owner Rene of the restaurant looked at me and said: "You are starting your journey as a chef, this is my first tip, it is very important and it should follow you for the years to come and if you decide to follow your path as chef. Buy a small notebook, something small but sturdy that fits into your pocket, in this book you write all recipes you have learnt, any combination of food you like, any recipe methods or techniques and any notes, so you can remember it for later."

Then, he reaches under the benches towards his knife draws, opens it, and takes a small black notebook. The notebook looked very old, used, greasy and fixed together with tape, suggesting it had seen it's fair share use and that it had been worn like an old pair of jeans. He added: "This is my first notebook, see I started this during my apprenticeship when I was 14 years old, and I am still using it now"

Well to Chef Rene, I listened, I observed and I followed. I do as you did and am still doing it now too, I carry my notebook with me and it is the first thing I tell all the chefs that work with me. With this idea,
I wanted to give something to others, a small tool they can use however and whenever they like. Making them develop and evolve, with new recipes they will love and hopefully share with their own family and friends or even carry on what a great Chef once told me to do.

CHEF'S TIPS

This chapter is a collection of small tips and explanations of terms. Very often for Chefs, we do not explain things in detail especially in the busy nature of a kitchen. Some things might be common sense for us, most of the time it is not common for everybody else. Therefore, I will try to make it a little bit easier to follow and understand.

Of course all these tips are based on my personal experiences, preferences, opinions and my own palate. I hope that after cooking your own recipe you will come up with your own tips, do not fear to try new things and do not fear to fail.

1. For any recipe you follow, for any recipe you will ever do and as a rule for all cooking: always taste! Always check the seasoning, taste is different to each and everyone. You have to season to your own taste as it is impossible to put exact quantities in a recipe. This is why I always put seasoning to taste in my recipes.

2. With a lot of fine dining recipes, and complicated dishes, there might be a lot of wastage. Be smart about it, plan and reuse the leftovers in other recipes or meals.

3. White or Black pepper? I like to use mainly white pepper, as it is milder. I only use black pepper for my meat on a nice steak or grilled tenderloin. I prefer black pepper to finish a dish, for example on a carbonara pasta or beef carpaccio.
I find the freshly cracked black pepper added to the last minute or even in front of your guests brings interest to their appetite.

4. To have nice finger foods you need nice serving platters, serving ware or canape dishes, I have recommended some of my favorite brands in the "Sourcing" chapter.

5. I have not put any portions per person as such. It always depends on the person and the occasion when you serve the canapes. I put the bite numbers so you have an idea on the number of pieces you will end up with per recipe. Everything depends on the type of event, the number of people and how many pieces you plan to serve each person.

6. All platters and produce I have been using have been sourced by professional hospitality suppliers. I will put a detailed list of all suppliers in the reference section. Please contact me on my Facebook page (*https://www.facebook.com/domesgourmet*) if you have any additional questions or concerns about any equipment, serving ware or the recipes, don't hesitate to send me a message.

7. For most of all recipes the 'methods' can be done a day before or earlier before serving time, in a professional kitchen this is usually called the "Mise en place", basically all the preparations that can be done before service.

8. And "plating-up", are all the steps to have all your finger food ready on your platter or tray, served to your guest as soon as possible.

9. 'Ras el Hanout' is a classic blend used in Moroccan cooking like tagines and spiced Couscous. The name means 'top of the shop' or the very best spice blend that a spice merchant (Souk) has to offer. You will most likely find a similar spice blend in your local grocer as 'Morocan Seasoning'.

10. Truffle paste is very expensive, you can find a cheaper alternative 'Tartufata'. It is an Italian recipe with truffles, combined with countryside mushrooms, cooked in olive oil with a touch of garlic and lightly seasoned with salt and pepper.

CHEF'S TIPS

11. What is a bain-marie?
    From the dictionary *www.dictionary.com* : "A receptacle containing hot or boiling water into which other containers are placed to warm or cook the food in them, or called double boiler." A bain marie is a water bath made by putting a pan or bowl of food over a pan of hot water which should be kept at just below boiling point. It is used to melt food or to keep delicate sauces and soups hot without further cooking, or for foods which spoil if cooked over a direct heat source.

12. What is a Rhodoid sheet?
    Rhodoid Sheets are rigid transparent PVC sheets with a very smooth surface, used to obtain pastry preparation or chocolate with a very glossy finish.

13. What is a Sabayon?
    Sabayon is an French creamy and rich dessert, or sometimes a beverage, made with eeg yolks, sugar, and a sweet wine. The dessert version is a light custard, whipped to incorporate a large amount of air. In France, it is called sabayon, while its Italian name is zabaione or zabaglione.

14. What is a Quenelle?
    As mentioned in *https://guide.michelin.com*, a quenelle is a perfectly smooth, rugby-ball scoop of any soft food that instantly upgrades your plating and gives dishes a sophisticated touch. At a fine-dining restaurant, you might see this technique used across dishes throughout your 10-course degustation: in a graceful oval scoop of pate atop a crisp baguette, displayed in a generous dollop of caviar or in a spoonful of tangy tapenade. It might be even more apparent at dessert when ice cream, mousse, whipped cream and sorbet are served in an elegant quenelle.

VEGETABLE

ASPARAGUS AND MUSHROOM
YIELD: 20 BITES

INGREDIENTS

Duxelles
- 100 grs bottom mushrooms
- 2 clove garlic
- 2 French Eschallots
- 2 sprig of thyme
- 2 tablespoon of white wine
- 1 lemon

Garnish
- 1 bunch thick green asparagus
- 1 bunch thick white asparagus
- EVOO
- Salt flakes
- Ground Cayenne pepper
- 10 pieces of edible flowers (violet, lavender, nasturtium, etc)

ASPARAGUS AND MUSHROOM
YIELD: 20 BITES

COOKING STEPS

Duxelles

1. Peel the eschallots and garlic, wash and rinse all ingredients
2. Put the mushrooms, garlic in a food processor or blender and blitz until puree.
3. Place this puree in a small saucepan and cook on small heat.
4. Add the chopped thyme, white wine and reduce until the puree become thick, "pasty", sticky.
5. Season with the cayenne, salt, a tablespoon of lemon juice and keep in the fridge.

Garnish

1. Have a medium pot of water ready on high heat, ready to boil.
2. Cut the asparagus tip (green and white), around 5 cm long.
3. Only keep the heads, the rest of the asparagus is perfect for a soup or fresh salad.
4. When the water is boiling, add 3 pinch of salt, the water needs to be well seasoned
5. First drop the white asparagus tips in the boiling
6. Leave them for about 3 minutes and take them out in ice cold water to cool.
7. Repeat the same operation with the green asparagus, keep the green ones a little bit crunchier than the white ones.
8. Once both asparagus are cold, take them out from the water, dry with kitchen tissue.

ASPARAGUS AND MUSHROOM
YIELD: 20 BITES

PLATING UP

1. Place the asparagus head on a large plate, if they keep rolling you can slightly trim the bottom of each head.
2. Sprinkle the heads with EVOO, cayenne, lemon zest and salt flakes.
3. Turn them over slightly so they are completely glazed by the oil and season, you just want to have them shiny, they should not be dripping oil.
4. Put the mushroom puree in a pastry piping bag and pipe a small line of puree on top of the asparagus head, from the tip of each head to the bottom, around 1-2 mm thick.
5. On each line of mushroom you can place a couple petals of flowers.
6. Add some more lemon zest and salt flakes on top of each asparagus.
7. Finally place each head delicately on your platter, don't hesitate to pat dry each asparagus on a kitchen tissue if you think they are wet or "oily" before placing on the serving platter.

BABY SPINACH FLAN AND RATATOUILLE

YIELD: 20-25 PIECES

INGREDIENTS

Flan
- 120 ml Full Milk
- 120 ml Pure Cream
- 12 x Whole eggs
- 240 g washed Baby Spinach leaves
- 6x peeled French Eshallots
- 50 g Ground Parmesan
- 2 pinch of ground Nutmeg
- Salt to taste

Ratatouille
- 1 Spanish (red) onion
- 1 green zucchini
- 1 medium size eggplant
- 1 red capsicum
- 4 tablespoons tomato sauce
- 2 tablespoons of tomato paste
- 1 teaspoon smoked paprika
- 4 leaves of basil
- 2 sprig of fresh thyme
- 100 ml olive oil
- 1 fresh pod of vanilla
- 50 ml white wine
- Salt to taste

Garnish
- 20x heads of Micro Basil
- Salt flakes

BABY SPINACH FLAN AND RATATOUILLE

YIELD: 20-25 PIECES

COOKING STEPS

Flan

1. Preheat the oven to 135c degrees.
2. Place all ingredients in a powerful blender (Nutribullet or stick blender).
3. Blend everything until smooth texture, make sure the mix does not heat up while mixing.
4. Poor the mix in a baking tray, around 15 cm x 25 cm. (better if the tray has straight edges) If you don't use a non stick baking tray, line the tray with baking paper, it will make it easier when the Flan is cold.
5. Bake at 135, without fan until the mixture is set, for approximately 25 to 35 minutes, depending on the size of the tray.
6. Once your flan is baked, take it out from the oven and let it cool down on the side. Check the center of the flan by stabbing it with the edge of a small knife. Nothing should be stuck to the blade.
7. When your flan is at room temperature, place the baking tray in the fridge for a couple hours, the flan needs to be very cold to be able to cut.

Ratatouille

1. Wash all vegetables and cut the onions, zucchini, eggplant and capsicum in 1/2 cm diced. (you can peel if you prefer, but I like to keep the skin)
2. Place a non-stick pan on the gas and add a splash of olive oil.
3. Start by adding the diced onion and thyme in the pan, cook them off for about 2 minutes on high heat.
4. Add the diced capsicum, diced eggplant and diced zucchini, and cook for another 2 minutes.
5. Then add the tomato sauce, tomato paste and paprika, reduce to low heat.
6. Mix everything gently together and add the wine to the vanilla. (cut the pod in half and scrap the grains from inside)
7. Cook it a little bit longer for another 2-3 minutes and season with the salt.
8. Turn the heat off and let it cool down for 10 minutes.
9. Taste if it needs more salt and place the ratatouille in a container for the fridge.

BABY SPINACH FLAN AND RATATOUILLE

YIELD: 20-25 PIECES

PLATING UP

1. Take the flan out from the fridge and place it on a cutting board.
2. The flan is usually nicer when turned upside down, as the bottom part is more flat and shiny.
3. Trim each side first to end up with a rectangle. The size should be around 15 cm x 25 cm.
4. The idea is to cut that rectangle into 3 bands of 5 cm each and each band into 8 pieces around 2-3 cm.
5. If you have good cutting skills and geometry, you should end up with individual pieces around 5x2.5cm. (given take)
6. Place all rectangle of flan on a tray and brush them with a little bit of olive oil until they shinny.
7. With a teaspoon, place a scoop of the cold ratatouille on top of the flans.
8. Finish with a pinch of salt flakes and a head of baby basil on each piece.

BABY VEG-GARDEN IN A GLASS

YIELD: 10 GLASSES

INGREDIENTS

Hummus
- 400 grs canned chickpeas
- 2 tablespoon tahini paste
- 4 cloves of peeled garlic
- 2 tablespoon of EVOO
- 4 lemon juice and zests
- 1 tablespoon smoking liquid
- 2 pinch of table salt

Garnish
- 10 x baby Dutch carrots
- 10 x baby yellow carrots
- 10 x green asparagus
- 10 x small long breakfast radish
- 1 tablespoon EVOO
- Salt flakes
- 1 tablespoon of sumac
- 10 pieces of edible flowers (violet, lavender, nasturtium…)

BABY VEG-GARDEN IN A GLASS

YIELD: 10 GLASSES

COOKING STEPS

Hummus

1. Open the canned chickpea and strain them, discard the liquid.
2. In a blender or food processor, place the drained chickpeas and all remaining hummus ingredients.
3. Blend all until smooth, you might need to shake the blender to help blend it. (you can add a little bit of cold water if your blender really struggles)
4. Check the seasoning and place in a container for the fridge

Veg

1. Place a medium pot full of water on the stove to be boiling.
2. Wash, peel the radishes, baby carrots and green asparagus.
3. Trim all above baby veg so they have roughly all the same size and length
4. When the pot of water is boiling add 3 pinch of table salt, then you can blanch the baby veg.
5. Start with the orange carrots first, for 2-3 minutes, as soon as they ready take them out form the boiling water and plunge them in cold ice water to stop them from cooking further. (you can cook them longer but I like to serve them still crunchy)
6. Then, repeat the same operation with the green asparagus and finally the yellow carrots. The yellow carrots are last as they color all the water yellow.
7. Once all your baby veg are cold, take them out from the ice water and dry them in a colander and kitchen tissue.

BABY VEG-GARDEN IN A GLASS

YIELD: 10 GLASSES

PLATING UP

1. This preparation should be served at room temperature, so make sure to take out all baby veg and hummus from the fridge early enough to give them time to come back to temperature. and not serving everything cold
2. Mix the hummus together and place in a plastic pastry bag.
3. Pipe the hummus in the small glass yogurt pots, ramequins or jars of your choices (about 3 cm high).
4. Sprinkle a little bit of sumac on top of each hummus.
5. Place all your vegetables flat on a large tray, drizzle some EVOO, sumac and salt flakes, roll all veg over so they shinny and season evenly.
6. Then, in each glass, stick a piece of orange carrot, a piece of yellow carrot, a head of asparagus and a piece of radish.
7. Keep the stems, leaf up, slightly coming out the glasses, it will be easier to grab for your guests.
8. Finally place a couple petals of edible flowers on the top of each vegetables to make it look nice.

BEETROOT AND GOATS CURD MARSHMALLOW

YIELD: 20-25 PIECES

INGREDIENTS

- 6 leaves Gelatine
- 75 g Egg white
- 25 g Glucose
- 250 g Caster sugar
- 125 g Beetroot puree
- 2 pinch of table salt
- 1 pinch ground black pepper
- 125 g Goats cheese
- 10 g Beetroot powder
- 75 g Water
- zest of 1 lemon

Garnish
- punnet baby chard

BEETROOT AND GOATS CURD MARSHMALLOW

YIELD: 20-25 PIECES

COOKING STEPS

1. Rehydrate the gelatine in ice water.
2. Mix the sugar, glucose and water in a medium pot.
3. Melt the sugar and heat sugar until 127 °C.
4. When the sugar reaches 127c turn the heat off and set aside.
5. Put the egg-white in a bowl and start whisking.
6. Off the gas, add the gelatine in the pot to the sugar mix. Be careful once the gelatine will melt it will foam a lot, that is why you need a large enough pot to keep everything from overflowing.
7. Make sure the gelatine is melted and pour it slowly into the egg-white that is still whisking.
8. The egg-white will double and be slightly cooked from the sugar.
9. Reduce the whisking speed and keep whisking until the mix is cold.
10. Take half of the marshmallow mix out from the bowl and separate it into a second bowl.
11. In the first half, add the beetroot puree, salt, pepper and beetroot powder.
12. In the second half add the goat cheese and lemon zest.
13. Lay out the beetroot marshmallow in the bottom of a tray lined up with baking paper.
14. Cool it down quickly, in the freezer for 5 minutes, to set the first layer.
15. Finally, add the second layer on top, with the goat cheese marshmallow mix.
16. Take the tray and hit it a couple times on top of the bench or tables, it will unify the layers and help remove some air bubbles.
17. Set the whole tray in the fridge overnight (around 6 hours).

BEETROOT AND GOATS CURD MARSHMALLOW

YIELD: 20-25 PIECES

PLATING UP

1. Take the marshmallow out from the fridge and place on the cutting board (with the baking paper).
2. Use a large knife and place it under hot water for 1 minute.
3. With the hot knife, trim each side of the marshmallow.
4. For each cut, heat up and wipe the knife to get a nice straight cut each slice.
5. Cut marshmallow around 1.5 cm square.
6. Finally, take a nice plate or long platter and place each cubes nicely on it.
7. Sprinkle with baby chard on top.

CURRIED CAULIFLOWER, TRUFFLE AND ZUCCHINI ROLLS

YIELD: 10-15 PIECES

INGREDIENTS

- 200 grs cauliflower
- 1 brown onion
- 1 teaspoon Agar-Agar powder
- Coconut cream
- 1 teaspoon Raz-El-Hanout Curry powder
- 1 teaspoon truffle paste
- 50 grs dry White wine
- 1 medium green zucchini
- 2 pinch table salt
- 2 tablespoon of olive oil

Garnish
- 5 pieces lavender flowers
- 2 tablespoon of EVOO
- 1 pinch of salt flakes

CURRIED CAULIFLOWER, TRUFFLE AND ZUCCHINI ROLLS

YIELD: 10-15 PIECES

COOKING STEPS

Curry creme

1. For this preparation you need a couple rhodoid plastic sheets and PVC small round tubes, 2cm thick, 10cm long.
2. Before we start, fill up the tubes with rhodoid sheets so that the Curry cream does not stick to the tubes.
3. If you don't have any pvc tubes or metal tubes, you can use a 4 colors BIC pen to roll the plastic around and keep it together with tape.
4. Take a large grater and grate the cauliflower in a large bowl.
5. Use a medium saucepan, add the olive oil and place on high heat.
6. When the oil is hot, pan fry the grated cauliflower.
7. Add the curry powder and pan fry for 3 minutes.
8. Then in the pan add the white wine and boil.
9. Reduce the white wine half way and add the coconut cream.
10. Add the Agar powder, mix well and boil for 2 minutes.
11. Turn the gas off and set aside.
12. Poor the coconut/ cauliflower mix in the plastic tub and set in the fridge for 3 hours.
13. When the tubes are sets, take them out form the fridge and remove delicately the wrapped plastic rhodoid.
14. Keep the coconut/ cauliflower tubes in the fridge.

For the cucumber

1. In a medium saucepan, fill it with water and place on high heat to boil.
2. Slice the zucchini around 2 millimeter thick.
3. When the water is boiler, put the sliced zucchini in the water for only 5 seconds.
4. Take them out from the water and cool them down straight away in ice water.
5. After 5 minutes take them out from the water and dry the zucchini.

CURRIED CAULIFLOWER, TRUFFLE AND ZUCCHINI ROLLS

YIELD: 10-15 PIECES

COOKING STEPS

1. In a medium saucepan, fill it with water and place on high heat to boil.
2. Slice the zucchini around 2 millimeter thick.
3. When the water is boiler, put the sliced zucchini in the water for only 5 seconds.
4. Take them out from the water and cool them down straight away in ice water.
5. After 5 minutes take them out from the water and dry the zucchini.
6. On the cutting board, cut the zucchini from the edge around 5 millimeter large with the green skin included, so they all look similar ribbons.
7. Then place the cut sliced zucchini one on top each other.
8. Start from the top skin facing down.
9. Continue by placing another one with just enough space to see a little bit of the white zucchini and still the skin facing down.
10. Keep repeating the method until you have enough zucchini ribbons to roll around a coconut/ cauliflower tubes.
11. Take a tube out from the fridge and place on top of the staked zucchini ribbons.
12. With a knife trim each side of the zucchini ribbons.
13. Finally, roll the zucchini ribbons around the coconut/ cauliflower tube (make sure it is tight).
14. Keep in the fridge.

CURRIED CAULIFLOWER, TRUFFLE AND ZUCCHINI ROLLS

YIELD: 10-15 PIECES

PLATING UP
1. Depending the size of your tube, usually you prefer to cut cut the tubes less than 5 cm long (bite size).
2. This recipe can be serve cold or warm.
3. I like to serve it warm, place the rolls on an oven tray and heat up at 100C for 5 minutes.
4. Place each wrapped tubes on individual spoons or on platters.
5. Drizzle a tiny bit of EVOO.
6. Place a couple petals on top of each tubes.
7. Finish with a little bit of salt flakes.

CRUMBED CAMEMBERT, CRANBERRY SALSA

YIELD: 20 PIECES

INGREDIENTS

Camembert
- 500 grs Camembert cheese (or any triple cream Brie cheese)
- 2 whole eggs
- 100 grs plain flour
- 200 grs bread crumbs
- 1 fresh nutmeg

Salsa
- 340 grs fresh (or frozen) cranberries
- 100 grs caster sugar
- 1 jalapeno , seeded and chopped coarsely (leave the seeds, if you like it spicy)
- 50 grs coriander
- 4 green onions
- 2 tablespoons lime juice
- 1 orange
- pinch of salt

CRUMBED CAMEMBERT, CRANBERRY SALSA

YIELD: 20 PIECES

COOKING STEPS

1. Take your Camembert and cut off all the crust.
2. Cut large cubes around 2 to 3 cm thick.
3. Place them on baking paper in the fridge, they have to be really cold (if the cheese is really soft you can put the cubes the freezer for 10 minutes).

Crumbing

1. With 3 large containers, one for the flour, one for the beaten eggs (called egg wash) and one for the crumbs.
2. In general any crumbing goes as follow, place a couple cubes in the flour and roll them until they covered with the flour, take they them out from the flour, dust the excess flour off and place in the egg wash.
3. Again roll the cubes in the egg wash, take them out one by one and drop them in the breadcrumbs.
4. Finally repeat the same operation, make sure the crumbs cover the entire cubes and try to keep the cubes as square as possible.

For the salsa

1. Pulse the cranberries and sugar together in a food processor or blender until cranberries are just roughly chopped.
2. Pour the cranberries into a medium bowl and stir in chopped jalapenos, chopped green onions, chopped fresh coriander and the zest and juice of the orange.
3. Cover the orange cranberry salsa and store in the refrigerator for at least 30 minutes to develop the flavors.

CRUMBED CAMEMBERT, CRANBERRY SALSA

YIELD: 20 PIECES

PLATING UP

1. Take the salsa and crumbed Camembert out form the fridge
2. Pre Heat the fryer to 200c (or oil in a deep pot)
3. The salsa will most likely have a lot of juices, so straining may be required
4. When the oil reaches the temperature, drop slowly the crumbed cheese in the hot oil, one by one, not more than five together.
5. After 3-4 minutes, the crumbled cheese should be ready: golden brown and crispy.
6. Take them out form the oil and place on kitchen paper to dry the leftover oil
7. Check that they all crispy and let them rest for a couple minutes
8. If you serve them straight away you might risk burning your mouth guests as the center is hot melted cheese.
9. Place the cheese cubes on a platter, you can serve the salsa in a small bowl on the side or place a small amount on each crumbed camembert, the choice is yours.

MACADAMIA DUXELLE TARTLET

YIELD: 20 PIECES

INGREDIENTS

- 20 mini savory round tartlet, around 41x17 mm
- 500 g button mushrooms
- 5 cloves of garlic
- 5 French shallots
- 2 sprig thyme
- 50 g Macadamia nuts
- 20 g parsley
- 20 g fresh tarragon
- 50 cl dry withe wine
- 1 teaspoon ground nutmeg
- 2 pinch of table salt
- 1 pinch Smokey paprika
- 10 cl of any vegetable oil
- 10 g salt flakes

Garnish
- 1 punnet of baby parsley
- 1 punnet of edible violet flowers
- OPTIONAL: marinated white anchovies

MACADAMIA DUXELLE TARTLET

YIELD: 20 PIECES

COOKING STEPS

1. First quickly rinse all ingredients, don't leave the mushrooms too long in water, they might absorb too much moisture.
2. Dry all ingredients before starting the recipe.
3. Chop all mushrooms with a large knife. Using a blender will puree too much the mushroom, for a duxelle it is better to use a knife to keep more texture for the end product. It is best to slice all mushrooms first then chopped, small amounts at each time.
4. Start cooking off all the chopped mushrooms, in a medium size pot on low heat add the oil with the mushrooms.
5. Chop the garlic, the french shallots and add them with the mushrooms.
6. With a large wooden spoon, keep scraping the bottom of the pot so the ingredients don't burn. You should see moisture coming out of the mushrooms. Keep cooking for another 10 minutes on low heat without giving too much color.
7. Chop all the herbs: thyme, parsley and tarragon as fine as possible and set aside for later
8. With the mushroom, add the nutmeg, salt, paprika and white wine.

PLATING UP

1. Put all empty tart shell on a tray.
2. With a small teaspoon, fill up all tarts.
3. Sprinkle a small pinch of salt flakes on top of the duxelle.
4. Finish with a couple violets or baby parsley to decorate.

MACADAMIA DUXELLE TARTLET
YIELD: 20 PIECES

PICKLED CUCUMBER AND GOATS CURD

YIELD: 20 PIECES

INGREDIENTS

- 3 medium Lebanese cucumber
- 100 grs goat curd
- 10 grs of fresh chives
- 10 grs of fresh Dill
- 2 piece of French shallots
- 1 lemon
- 2 pinch of ground native mountain pepper
- 2 sheets Brick pastry
- ½ cup of white balsamic vinegar

Pickling liquid
- ½ cup water
- 1 tablespoon of white sugar
- 1 teaspoon coriander seeds
- 30 grs olive oil

Garnish
- the tops of the dill
- 1 punnet marigold flower

PICKLED CUCUMBER AND GOATS CURD

YIELD: 20 PIECES

COOKING STEPS

For the filling

1. On a cutting board, slice the chives as thin as possible and chop the dill (keep the nice top for Garnish).
2. Dice the shallots as small as possible, keep the trimming for the pickling liquid.
3. In a medium size bowl, put the goat's curd, shallots, chives and chopped dill.
4. Give it a good mix and add the juice and zest of one lemon.
5. Finish with the ground mountain pepper, mix well and keep in the fridge for plate up.

Pickling liquid

1. In a small pot, put the balsamic, water, vinegar, coriander seeds and shallot trimmings.
2. Mix all together and boil everything.
3. Turn the heat off as soon as it boil and set aside.
4. Peel all cucumber and slice them about 1,5 cm thick.
5. WIth a tiny round cutter, cut the center of each cucumber slice.
6. Keep all rings in a small container and cover them with the pickling liquid.
7. Put the container in the fridge overnight.

PICKLED CUCUMBER AND GOATS CURD

YIELD: 20 PIECES

COOKING STEPS

For the brick

1. Pre-heat the oven to 130c.
2. Take an oven tray and cover it with baking paper.
3. On the paper, place one sheet of Brick and brush it with the olive oil.
4. Put the second sheet of Brick on top of the first one and brush with some oil again.
5. Place another sheet of baking paper on top of the Brick and put another tray on top.
6. Placing the Brick between 2 trays keeps the Brick flat.
7. Bake the Brick in the oven for 20 minutes. The Brick has to be lightly golden and crispy.
8. Leave them another 5-10 minutes if they are not hard enough.
9. Once you take them out from the oven, let them cool down and dry them on kitchen tissue if they are too oily.

PLATING UP

1. Take the cucumber out the fridge and drain the rings from the liquid.
2. On a tray place half of all Brick squares.
3. On top of each square place a ring of pickled cucumber.
4. With a teaspoon, fill up the rings with the goat's mix, fill it up high enough to be able to stick another Brick.
5. Cover all cucumber with the rest of the Brick squares.
6. Place the cucumber rings upwards, standing up on your serving platter.
7. Place a piece of dill or flowers on top to finish.

PORCINI, KALE AND PINE-NUTS SPRING ROLLS

YIELD: 12 PIECES

INGREDIENTS

- 100grs Kale
- 100grs Ricotta cheese
- 2 tablespoon olive oil
- 2 clove of garlic
- 1 lemon
- 5grs dried Porcini mushroom
- 2 tablespoon of Pine Nuts
- 4 sheet of Filo pastry
- 2 eggs
- table salt
- ground white pepper

PORCINI, KALE AND PINE-NUTS SPRING ROLLS

YIELD: 12 PIECES

COOKING STEPS

Filling

1. Wash the garlic and kale and slice them both up.
2. Put the dried mushroom in a fruit blender or spice blender and reduce it to powder.
3. In a pan add the oil and garlic.
4. Cook it for 2-3 minutes and add the sliced kale.
5. Cook all for another 5 minutes and add the porcini powder.
6. Add the juice and zest from the lemon and turn the heat off.
7. In a medium bowl, put the ricotta cheese, the cooked. kale, the pine nuts and 1 egg
8. Season it the with the salt, white pepper and mix well.

Spring roll

1. Lay down the Filo pastry flat on a bench.
2. Put the last egg in a small bowl, add a pinch of salt and whisk it with a fork (this is the egg wash).
3. With a brush, cover some egg wash all over the filo pastry.
4. Place another sheet of filo on top, and brush more egg wash.
5. Cut the filo pastry in 6 equal squares.
6. On each squares put one full spoon of filling.
7. Roll the filo up, bottom first to cover the filling, then add each side and finish rolling it.
8. Place each roll on baking paper on a tray, in the fridge.

PORCINI, KALE AND PINE-NUTS SPRING ROLLS

YIELD: 12 PIECES

PLATING UP

1. Pre-heat the fryer to 180c and take the spring roll out from the fridge.
2. When the oil reaches the temperature, drop slowly the rolls in the hot oil, one by one, not more than five together.
3. After 3-4 minutes, the rolls should be ready: golden brown and crispy.
4. Take them out form the oil and place on kitchen paper to dry the leftover oil.
5. Place the rolls on platter and serve straight away.

POTATO AND TRUFFLE CROQUETTE

YIELD: 15-20 PIECES

POTATO AND TRUFFLE CROQUETTE

YIELD: 15-20 PIECES

INGREDIENTS

- 300grs Desiree Potato
- 5x Egg
- 2 tablespoon Truffle paste
- 50grs shredded Comte cheese (or Gruyere Cheese)
- 50grs shredded Mozzarella
- 1 teaspoon ground Nutmeg
- 1 teaspoon table salt
- 50grs plain flour
- 100grs breadcrumbs
- 3 sprigs fresh lemon thyme

Garnish
- punnet of baby radishes cress
- OPTIONAL: salmon caviar

COOKING STEPS

Croquette

1. Take the fresh Thyme, remove all small leaves from the stem and chop very fine, set aside.
2. In a large pot, put all the potatoes and cover them with water, place the pot on high heat.
3. Boil until cooked, you should be able to stick a knife in the potato and the potato will slowly slide off the knife: this means the potato are done.
4. Take them out form the water and let them cool down for 10 minutes.
5. Peel all potato and put them in a large mixing bowl.
6. Add the chopped thyme, Egg yolks, nutmeg, salt, truffle paste, Comte and Mozzarella shredded cheeses.
7. With a potato masher or a large wooden spoon and mash all the potatoes.
8. Mix well and place in a plastic piping bag with a straight pastry nozzle 10mm thick.
9. On a flat tray, cover it with cling wrap and pipe the potato mix from one side to the other.
10. Leave around 1 cm space and pipe another line of potato horizontally.
11. Repeat the process until all potato mix is piped.
12. With a large knife cut the lines vertically, around 5 cm wide.
13. Leave all potato mix on the tray, don't move them, portioning the potato mix will give the potato croquette it final shape.

POTATO AND TRUFFLE CROQUETTE

YIELD: 15-20 PIECES

COOKING STEPS

Croquette

14. Place all trays in freezer until frozen hard
15. When the potato mix logs are hard you can take them off the tray.
16. You can store them frozen as they are now in zip log bag if required.

Crumbing

1. With 3 large containers, one for the flour, one for the leftover egg white and one for the crumbs.
2. In general any crumbing goes as follow, place a couple potato logs in the flour and roll them until they covered with the flour, take they them out from the flour, dust the excess flour off and place in the egg wash.
3. Again roll the logs in the egg wash, take them out one by one and drop them in the breadcrumbs.
4. Finally repeat the same operation, make sure the crumbs cover the entire logs, and your croquettes are ready to fry (you can store them back in the freezer with the crumbing, but they are more fragile).

POTATO AND TRUFFLE CROQUETTE
YIELD: 15-20 PIECES

PLATING UP

1. Heat up the fryer at 200 degree Celsius.
2. Take the croquette out from the freezer, it is better to let the croquette slightly come up in temperature, so you will not end up with a frozen center croquette.
3. When the oil is hot place the croquette in the frying basket a drop them in the oil.
4. If you have done your crumbing properly and not too thick, it should take around 5 minutes to fry, the crust should be golden brown crispy.
5. Take them out from the oil and place them on a kitchen paper to absorb the residual oil.
6. Leave them for 5 minutes to cool down so they not burning your guests mouth with melted cheese.
7. Place them on a tray or plate.
8. Put a little bit of salmon caviar and garnish on top.

TOMATO AND STRAWBERRY GAZPACHO
YIELD: 10 PORTIONS

TOMATO AND STRAWBERRY GAZPACHO

YIELD: 10 PORTIONS

INGREDIENTS

- 200grs ripe strawberry
- 400grs ripe truss tomato
- 2 cloves of garlic
- 1 telegraph cucumber
- 1 Spanish onion
- -1 slice of white bread
- 2 tablespoon red wine vinegar
- 2 tablespoon soy sauce
- 50 ml EVOO
- 1 red capsicum
- 1 stem of celery
- 1 pinch paprika
- 2 pinch table salt
- 100 ml mineral water

Garnish
- 5 celery leaves
- -2 truss tomato
- 20 grs of chives
- 1 lemon

COOKING STEPS

1. Only peel the garlic and onions.
2. Wash and rinse all other ingredients: strawberry, tomato, capsicum, celery, cucumber.
3. Remove the seeds form the capsicum.
4. Cut the onion, capsicum, cucumber and celery in half.
5. Place all vegetables in a large blender and add all the other ingredients (except garnish).
6. Blend all until completely smooth.
7. Poor all in a container and leave in the fridge overnight.

PLATING UP

1. Take the gazpacho out from the fridge and with a fine mesh strainer, strain the gazpacho.
2. Add a tablespoon of lemon juice and taste the gazpacho.
3. Adjust the seasoning to your liking.
4. Keep the gazpacho chilled until serving.
5. Dice all garnish, celery, tomato and chives.
6. To serve you can use small shot glasses or small glass yogurt pots.
7. Fill up the glasses halfway.
8. In each glass, sprinkle a little bit of the cut garnishes: celery leaves, diced tomato and chopped chives.
9. Finish with the zest of the lemon and served immediately.

THYME, FETA AND ONION MINI QUICHES

YIELD: 12 PIECES

INGREDIENTS

- 4 sprig fresh thyme
- 4 brown onion
- 2 tablespoon veg oil
- 50 grs balsamic vinegar
- 4 eggs
- 200 ml cream
- 200 ml milk
- 3 pinch table salt
- 2 pinch white pepper
- 3 sheets puff pastry

THYME, FETA AND ONION MINI QUICHES

YIELD: 12 PIECES

COOKING STEPS

Caramelized onion
1. Slice all onions and pan fry them in a large non-stick pan with the oil.
2. For about 5 minutes, keep stirring the onions.
3. Add the balsamic vinegar and reduce slightly.
4. Caramelize the onion until they have a nice light brown color and no more liquid.
5. Turn the heat off and set the caramelized onion aside.

Egg filling
1. Take the fresh Thyme, remove all small leaves from the stem and chop very fine.
2. In a mixing bowl, place the eggs, cream, milk, chopped thyme, pepper and salt.
3. Mix all well using a whisk.

Quiches
1. Pre-heat the oven to 200c.
2. Using a canola cooking spray, spray your muffin tin to prevent the quiches to stick after baking.
3. Take the 3 sheets of puff pastry and cut them in 4 equal squares.
4. Place each square in medium size muffin tray.
5. With your fingers, push down the dough down each muffin mold.
6. In the bottom of each quiches, divide equally the caramelized onion.
7. Take the feta cheese and break it up in smaller pieces.
8. Place the smaller pieces on the caramelized onion, around 10grs per quiches.
9. Put the muffin tray in the oven.
10. Take your egg filling and poor it in each muffin mold (while in the oven).

THYME, FETA AND ONION MINI QUICHES

YIELD: 12 PIECES

COOKING STEPS

Quiches

11. Pouring the mix while the tray is in the oven is a lot easier as you don't have to carry the tray full with egg mix (make sure you don't burn yourself).
12. Fill up each tart as much as possible.
13. Close the oven door and turn the temperature down to 180c.
14. The quiches should take around 15 minutes to bake.
15. Once they are cooked take them out form the oven and allow them to cool down for 10 minutes before serving.

PLATING UP

1. The quiches can be baked earlier, cool them down and keep in the fridge.
2. It will only take 5 minutes in a 170c oven to reheat.
3. Places them on a nice platter or keep it rustic and serve them in their own baking tray.
4. They go really well with a nice tomato relish.

THYME, FETA AND ONION MINI QUICHES

YIELD: 12 PIECES

WATERMELON AND MOZZARELLA SKEWERS
YIELD: 15 PIECES

INGREDIENTS

Salsa Verde
- 2 cloves garlic
- 10 pieces green shallots
- ½ bunch of fresh continental parsley
- ½ bunch of fresh mint
- ½ bunch of fresh coriander
- 1 small handful of capers
- ½ cup orange juice
- 3 tablespoons rice wine vinegar
- 8 tablespoons EVOO

For the skewers
- ½ small seedless watermelon
- 15x Vinegar Pearl onions
- 2 tablespoon Pomegranate Glaze
- 15x Cherry Bocconcini Mozzarella
- EVOO
- a couple sprigs of parsley

Pickling liquid
- 50grs Red wine vinegar
- 50grs sugar
- 50grs water
- 50grs Balsamic Vinegar

WATERMELON AND MOZZARELLA SKEWERS

YIELD: 15 PIECES

COOKING STEPS

Salsa verde
1. Peel the garlic and wash all herbs.
2. In a blender put the garlic, shallots, herbs, capers, orange juice, rice vinegar and oil.
3. Blend until the salsa is very smooth and free of chunks.
4. Keep in the fridge for at least 30 minutes.

Pickling liquid
1. In a small saucepan, put the red wine vinegar, sugar, water and balsamic.
2. Mix well to dissolve the sugar and place on high heat.
3. When the pickling liquid is boiling, turn the heat off.
4. OPTIONAL: You can add herbs or spices in your hot pickling liquid to bring more interesting flavours: like star anise and dill or mint and cinnamon.
5. Put the liquid in a large container and cool it down in fridge.
6. Take the watermelon and dice cubes 2,5cm square.
7. Put all watermelon cubes in the pickling liquid.
8. Let them marinated at least 12 hours.

WATERMELON AND MOZZARELLA SKEWERS

YIELD: 15 PIECES

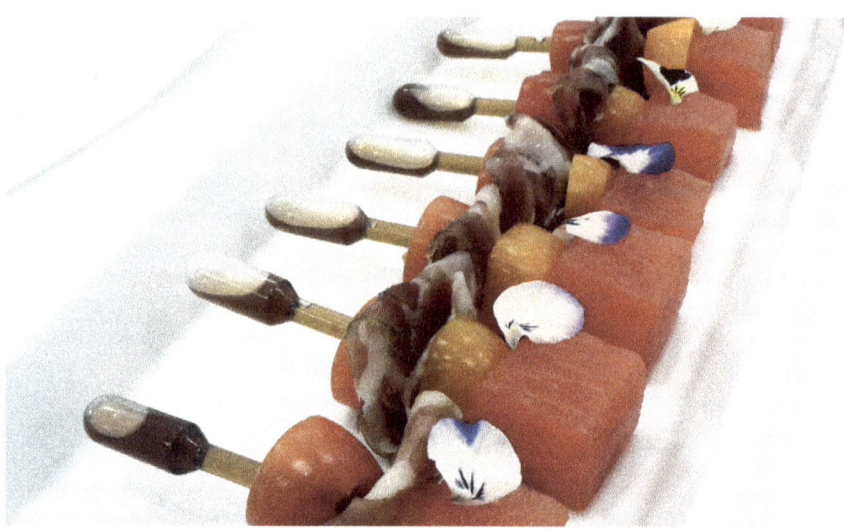

PLATING UP

1. First fill up the plastic pipettes.
2. Drain your pickled watermelon and save the liquid in another container.
3. Squeeze your pipette to remove all air.
4. Keep it squeezed and plunge the pipette into the watermelon liquid.
5. As you release the pressure, the pipette will fill itself with the liquid.
6. Repeat this operation until all pipettes are full
7. Drain the bocconcini and pearl onions.
8. In a small mixing bowl, put all pearl onions and the pomegranate glaze.
9. Mix them until all onion are glazed with the pomegranate.
10. Start putting the garnishes on the pipettes.
11. Take your pipette and stick a piece of watermelon until the end.
12. Then add a piece of pearl onion and finish with a piece of bocconcini.
13. Stack them all on a nice plate or tray.
14. With a teaspoon, place some dots of salsa verde around the skewers.
15. Finish with a couple pieces of parsley.

SEAFOOD

COFFEE CURD KINGFISH AND CRANBERRY

YIELD: 20 PIECES

COFFEE CURD KINGFISH AND CRANBERRY

YIELD: 20 PIECES

INGREDIENTS

Cured fish
- 250grs caster sugar
- 500grs table salt
- 50grs fresh ground coffee
- 3 lemons
- 1 side of Kingfish Hiramasa

Cranberry gel
- 200 grs frozen cranberry
- ½ teaspoon Xanthana Gum powder
- 50grs maple syrup

Garnish
- 1 ruby red grapefruit
- 1 bunch breakfast radishes
- 1 punnet baby coriander
- 50grs EVOO

COOKING STEPS

Curing

1. Trim the Kingfish and remove all skin.
2. Remove all the blood, cut in half, so you left only with two long fillet.
3. For the curing mix: In a bowl, mix the salt, sugar, the zest of the lemons and the ground coffee.
4. Place a large piece of aluminium foil on your bench.
5. Cover it with ⅓ of your curing mix, place the kingfish on top.
6. Cover the kingfish completely with the left-over curing mix.
7. Wrap up the aluminum foil and place it in the fridge.

COFFEE CURD KINGFISH AND CRANBERRY

YIELD: 20 PIECES

COOKING STEPS

Curing

8. Let it cure for at least 24 hours.
9. Finally take the foil out from the fridge, open it and take out the kingfish.
10. You can slice a small piece of fish and taste it to be sure you happy with the curing time.
11. It is possible to leave it for another 24 hours, the longer you cure the fish the more coffee and salty the fish will become.
12. When you are happy with the fish, delicately rinse the salt off the kingfish (make sure the water is cold).
13. Pat dry the Kingfish and store in dry container in the fridge.

Cranberry

1. Defrost the cranberry.
2. Juice the 3 lemons you used for the curing mix.
3. In a blender, put the cranberry, lemon juice, xanthana and maple syrup.
4. Blend until completely smooth, put in a squeeze bottle and keep in the fridge.

Garnish

1. Peel and segment the grapefruit, then cut each segment in small piece around 1 cm.
2. Put all grapefruit in a container with the juice in the fridge.
3. Slice the radishes into small batons, keep also in the fridge.

COFFEE CURD KINGFISH AND CRANBERRY

YIELD: 20 PIECES

PLATING UP

1. Prepare the white Chinese ceramic soup spoons, line them up next to each other on your bench.
2. Slice all the kingfish fish, slightly on an angle, about 1 mm thick.
3. Place 2 slices on each spoon, slightly curved up to give the food some "height".
4. With the squeeze bottle, put 2 dots of cranberry gel.
5. Add 2 small pieces of grapefruit and a piece of baby coriander on top.
6. Finally, drizzle a little bit of the grapefruit juice and EVOO on top of the kingfish to make it shinny.

CRAB AND PRAWN TORTELLINI
YIELD: 20 PIECES

CRAB AND PRAWN TORTELLINI

YIELD: 20 PIECES

INGREDIENTS

Tortellini
- 170grs crabmeat
- 200grs prawn cutlets (tails)
- 20grs grated ginger
- 50grs garlic chives(or green onion)
- 30grs soy sauce
- 2 tbs sesame oil
- 4 cloves garlic
- 1 tomato
- 1/2 packed of Chinese wonton wrapper
- 2 eggs

Brown butter sauce
- 200 grs unsalted butter
- 1 lemon
- 2 sprig of sage
- 2 pinch table salt

Garnish
- 50grs salt flakes
- 1 punnet baby radishes
- 3 tablespoon of EVOO
- 2 pinch of Salt Flakes

COOKING STEPS

Tortellini

1. Chop the garlic, ginger and garlic chives.
2. Cut the tomato into quarter, remove the center so you left with 4 tomato petals
3. Dice those petals around 5 mm thick.
4. Take all prawns and remove all shell and tails
5. Put them on a chopping board and roughly chop them.
6. In a large mixing bowl, put all ingredients together: the prawn, the crabmeat, chopped garlic, ginger and chives, the diced tomato, the soy and sesame oil
7. Mix well, and keep in the fridge for 3 hours before using.
8. Take your mix and wonton wrapper out from the fridge.
9. Do 3-4 tortellini at the time, if you put too many wonton wrappers on your bench they will dry out very quickly. (keep you wonton stack covered with a wet towel)
10. Put the eggs in a small bowl and mix well.
11. Place 3 wonton wrappers on your bench.
12. With a brush, cover the edges of each wonton with the beaten eggs.
13. Use a small teaspoon and place a small amount of prawn mix in the center of the wonton.

CRAB AND PRAWN TORTELLINI

YIELD: 20 PIECES

COOKING STEPS

Tortellini

14. Fold the wonton together from one side to the other to obtain a triangle
15. Make sure your wonton is perfectly sealed without any air bubbles.
16. Then, take each side of the triangle (left and right) and fold them together to form the tortellini.
17. Keep each tortellini on a tray, on top of baking paper to prevent them from sticking to each other.
18. Repeat the same process until you have used all prawn mix.
19. Keep the tortellini in the fridge under cling wrap.

Brown Butter sauce

1. The basic idea of brown butter is to cook the milk solid from the butter.
2. First, cut the butter into large cubes.
3. In a medium saucepan, put the butter and place it on high heat.
4. Let the butter melt completely.
5. After melting the butter will start bubbling and cooking.
6. You should start to see some milky white content coming up with the milk solid from the butter.
7. Continue cooking this solid until the butter starts becoming brown.
8. Reduce your heat to medium as it can go very fast and burn your butter.
9. You want to try caramelizing the milk solid without burning.
10. The secret is to use your nose: when you butter starts cooking, you should start smelling a nutty smell, become stronger the more you cook your butter.
11. When your butter has a light brown color and nutty smell turn off the heat.
12. Add the juice of the lemon and the sage straight in the brown butter.
13. Be careful, adding juice that is basically water, in brown butter, that is basically hot fat: the result is the fat will foam and explode.

CRAB AND PRAWN TORTELLINI

YIELD: 20 PIECES

COOKING STEPS

Brown Butter sauce

14. Use a large whisk to mix very quickly and have your juice in a jug to quickly pour it in.
15. If you are not confident, use a probe and take your butter up to 140c and stop the cooking by adding the juice.
16. Once your brown butter is done, add the salt and leave aside to cool down.
17. Brown butter can be stored in the fridge but is better to be done fresh for each day.

PLATING UP

1. Place a large pot of salted water on the gas, on high heat.
2. Place all your chinese spoon on a serving tray
3. Take the tortellini out from the fridge, so they come back to temperature and they are not too cold.
4. If your Brown butter is hard cold, put it in a plastic bowl and melt it in the microwave for 40 seconds.
5. When the water is boiling, drop half of the tortellini (if your pot is big enough you can cook all at once!)
6. If your water was really boiling, it should take the tortellini around 6-8 minutes.
7. Take out the tortellini from the water and place them in a large bowl.
8. Repeat the same process with the other half of the tortellini.
9. Drizzle the EVOO and add the salt flakes on top of all the tortellini.
10. Gently mix the tortellini to coat them with the salt and oil.
11. Place one tortellini in each spoon.
12. Drizzle one tablespoon of warm brown butter over each tortellini.
13. Finish with some baby radish and serve immediately.

CRISPY PRAWN
YIELD: 20 PIECES

CRISPY PRAWN
YIELD: 20 PIECES

INGREDIENTS

- 20x Prawn cutlets (Jumbo 16/20)
- 20 large leaf of Basil
- 5 sheet of Brick pastry
- 1 Egg

Chilli sauce
- *100grs of tomato ketchup*
- *100grs whole Egg Mayonnaise*
- *1 tablespoon smoked paprika*
- *1 tablespoon Cognac (French Brandy)*

COOKING STEPS

1. Peel all prawns, the heads can be discarded and the tails, shell removed.
2. Clean and devein the tails.
3. Crack the egg and put in a small bowl.
4. With a fork, beat the egg up.
5. Make sure your bench is cleaned, if necessary, cover it with cling wrap.
6. Take one sheet of Brick pastry and cut it in quarters.
7. Place each quarter next to each other, the "pointy right angle" facing yourself.
8. On each "pointy right angle", place a basil leaf.
9. Then, on top of each leaf, place a prawn tail.
10. With a brush, cover each "round" top of Brick pastry with the Beaten egg wash.
11. Finally, roll each quarter up, from bottom (right angle) to the round top.
12. Take a small toothpick and stick it thru every rolled brick/prawn to keep all together.
13. Store them on baking paper in the fridge.
14. It is recommended to roll the prawn in the brick on the same day you like to serve them (After 24 hours, the moisture of the tails will ruin the brick pastry).

Chilli sauce
1. In a small bowl, put all ingredients.
2. Mix well and keep in the fridge.

CRISPY PRAWN
YIELD: 20 PIECES

PLATING UP

1. Pre-heat the fryer to 200c (or a large pot filled with canola oil).
2. Make sure your rolled prawn and sauce are out from the fridge.
3. In your serving tray place some baking paper in the bottom, then place a glass in the middle.
4. Fill up the glass with the sauce.
5. When the oil is at temperature, drop the rolled prawns in it.
6. Don't put all together, if too many they will stick together.
7. It works best when they drop one after the other and probably 5 per basket.
8. They will cook quickly, after 3 minutes they should be light golden brown and crispy.
9. Take them out from the oil and place them on kitchen paper.
10. Finally place them around the glass on the tray.

CURED OCEAN TROUT AND AVOCADO
YIELD: 15-20 PIECES

CURED OCEAN TROUT AND AVOCADO

YIELD: 15-20 PIECES

INGREDIENTS

Curing mix
- 2250grs caster sugar
-500grs table salt
-1 bunch of dill
-3 lemons
-1 side of Trout

Avocado cream
- 4 ripe avocado
-50grs soy milk
-a pinch table salt
-1x lemon

Puffed wild rice
- 50 grs Wild Rice
-200 ml canola oil
-salt to taste

Garnish
- a handful wild rice
-5 violet flowers

CURED OCEAN TROUT AND AVOCADO

YIELD: 15-20 PIECES

COOKING STEPS

Curing

1. Wash and rinse the dill.
2. Roughly chop it and set aside.
3. Trim the Trout and remove all skin.
4. Remove all the blood, cut in half, so you left only with two long fillets
5. For the curing mix: In a bowl, mix the salt, sugar, the zest of the lemons and the dill.
6. Place a large piece of aluminum foil on your bench
7. Cover it with ⅓ of your curing mix, place the Trout on top.
8. Cover the Trout completely with the leftover curing mix.
9. Wrap up the aluminum foil and place it in the fridge.
10. Let it cure for at least 24 hours.
11. Finally take the foil out from the fridge, open it and take out the Trout.
12. You can slice a small piece of fish and taste it to be sure you are happy with the curing time.
13. It is possible to leave it for another 24 hours, the longer you cure the fish the more flavoured and salty the fish will become.
14. When you are happy with the fish, delicately rinse the salt off the Trout (make sure the water is cold).
15. Pat dry the Trout and store in a dry container in the fridge.

Avocado cream

1. Make sure your avocado is soft and ripe.
2. Cut the avocado in half and remove the seed and peel them.
3. Place the half avocados in a blender, add the soy milk, salt and the juice of the lemon.
4. Blend all until smooth but keep it short, if you blend for too long the blender will heat the avocado and you might lose the green color from the avocado.
5. Discard the avocado cream in a plastic piping bag and keep in the fridge.

CURED OCEAN TROUT AND AVOCADO

YIELD: 15-20 PIECES

COOKING STEPS

Puffed wild rice

1. Put the canola oil in a medium size pot.
2. Turn the heat on full, the oil needs to become really hot, almost smoking.
3. As soon as it starts smoking, drop the wild rice in the oil and turn the heat off.
4. Mix the oil gently to make all wild rice pop up.
5. Then take the rice out from the oil and place it on kitchen paper.
6. Season the rice with table salt and keep dry in a box.

PLATING UP

1. Place all spoons on your tray ready for plate up.
2. Cut the cured Trout in small cubes of about 2 cm squares.
3. Put one square per spoon.
4. With the avocado cream, pipe a small amount of avocado on top of the Trout.
5. Finish with a little bit of puffed rice and a petal of flowers on the avocado.

MORETON BAY BUG WRAPPED IN BETEL LEAF
YIELD: 20 PIECES

INGREDIENTS

- 10x whole medium Moreton Bay Bug

Garnish
- 20x betel leaf
- 5x fresh Kaffir lime leaves
- 50grs fried shallots
- 20 pieces of crispy pork rind

Sauce Ginger
- 50grs Sriracha
- 100grs whole Egg Mayonnaise
- 2 tablespoon Pickled ginger
- 1 tablespoon Pickled ginger juice
- 2 tablespoon Sesame oil
- 1 Lime

MORETON BAY BUG WRAPPED IN BETEL LEAF

YIELD: 20 PIECES

COOKING STEPS

1. Place a large pot of salted water on the gas, on high heat.
2. When the water is boiling, drop the Moreton bay in the water.
3. Cook them for 6 minutes.
4. Take them out and from the water and drop them in ice cold water to stop them from cooking.
5. After around 10 minutes, take the bugs out of the water and remove the tails from the head.
6. On a cutting board, cut the Moreton bug tails in half.
7. Remove the tails meat from the shell and discard the shell.
8. Keep the tails in the fridge.

Sauce ginger

1. In a blender, place the sriracha, oil, ginger, ginger juice and the juice and zest of the lime
2. Blend for one minute and discard the mix in a medium mixing bowl.
3. In this mix, add the mayonnaise and mix well.
4. Keep the sauce in the fridge.

Garnish

1. Stack all the kaffir leaves on top of each other, with a knife, slice the leaf as thin as possible.

MORETON BAY BUG WRAPPED IN BETEL LEAF

YIELD: 20 PIECES

PLATING UP

1. Lay down all betel leaves on a large cleaned bench.
2. Put half a tablespoon of the sauce on each betel leaf.
3. Place half of the bug tails on the sauce.
4. Add a little bit of sauce on top.
5. Sprinkle some fried shallot and crispy pork on top of the tails.
6. Finish with some sliced Kaffir leaves.

OYSTER WITH CHAMPAGNE AND COCONUT FOAM

YIELD: 24 PIECES

OYSTER WITH CHAMPAGNE AND COCONUT FOAM

YIELD: 24 PIECES

INGREDIENTS

- 2 dozen of Sydney Rock Oysters
- -1 tablespoon salt flakes
- -1 teaspoon Espelette pepper (or Cayenne pepper)

Foam
- 300ml Champagne
- 400ml Coconut Milk
- 4 leaves of gelatines
- 1/2 lime
- 1 tablespoon of Fish sauce

COOKING STEPS

Foam

1. Put the gelatine in cold water to rehydrate for 10 minutes.
2. Use a small saucepan and heat up the coconut milk.
3. When the coconut is hot, add the gelatine and melt it.
4. Pour the mix in a medium bowl.
5. Add the Champagne, fish sauce and juice of half a lime.
6. Give a good mix and pour it in a Siphon cream whipper.
7. Add one charge of N2O creamer.
8. Give the bottle a shake and place it in the fridge for at least 6 hours.

PLATING UP

1. Open the oyster as close to serving time as possible.
2. Make sure they are fresh and that they don't smell bad. Eating dead oyster can get you very sick.
3. Place the Oyster on a tray.
4. Take out the Siphon from the fridge and add another N2O charge in it.
5. Strongly shake the Siphon and test it out to make sure the foam comes out nicely.
6. Put a small amount of foam on top of each Oyster.
7. Finish with a sprinkle of pepper on top of the foam.
8. You should serve them with small toothpicks or tea forks to help eating.
9. As the foam will not last forever you should serve the Oysters as soon as possible.

PAN FRIED SCALLOP, PEAR AND BLACK GARLIC

YIELD: 20 PIECES

PAN FRIED SCALLOP, PEAR AND BLACK GARLIC

YIELD: 20 PIECES

INGREDIENTS

- 20x Sea Scallop (no shell, no roe)
- 4 tablespoon of unsalted butter
- canola oil
- table salt and white pepper to season

Black Garlic
- 100 grs peeled garlic cloves
- 2 bay leaves
- 1 tablespoon skid ink
- 1 tablespoon COLD unsalted butter
- a pinch table salt

Garnish
- 3 Corella Pear
- 4 tablespoon mirin
- 4 tablespoon soy sauce
- 6 tablespoon sesame oil
- 1 punnet Baby Shiso cress

COOKING STEPS

Black garlic

1. Place the peeled garlic cloves and bay leaf in a small pot, cover it with cold water and place on high heat.
2. When the water is boiling, turn the heat on low and let it simmer for about 2 minutes.
3. With the tip of a knife check that the garlic is cooked and soft.
4. Strain the garlic.
5. Straight away put the cooked garlic in a blender, add the skid ink, salt and COLD butter.
6. Blend all for about 30 second, not too long, just enough to get a smooth texture with no lumps.
7. You should not need seasoning as the skid ink is already salty, but it is always good to taste so you are happy with the taste.
8. Discard in a plastic container and place in the fridge.

Garnish

1. In a small bowl, mix the mirin, soy and sesame oil, keep this dressing aside.
2. Peel and dice all pear.
3. Put all diced pear in a medium bowl, 4 tablespoon of the dressing and mix well.

PAN FRIED SCALLOP, PEAR AND BLACK GARLIC

YIELD: 20 PIECES

PLATING UP

1. Take all your ingredients to room temperature, especially the Scallops.
2. Place all your spoons on a bench.
3. Cook the scallops just before serving them, the closer you can cook them to serving, the better texture and taste they will be, for this recipe I recommend pan frying the scallop 10 minutes before serving.
4. Place a medium non-stick pan on high heat.
5. Make sure the scallops are pat dry and season them with salt and pepper.
6. When the pan is hot, add a good drizzle of canola oil.
7. Directly put the scallop in the pan, probably only 10 at the time.

PAN FRIED SCALLOP, PEAR AND BLACK GARLIC

YIELD: 20 PIECES

8. You should see the scallop searing straight away otherwise your pan was not hot enough.
9. The cooking should be very fast altogether, cook the scallops for 1-2 minute until you have a nice golden brown crust.
10. Flip all scallop and do the other side for another 1-1/2 minute.
11. When the scallops are cooked, take them out from the pan and place on a kitchen paper.
12. You can repeat the same operation with the other 10 remaining Scallops.
13. In the same pan you used to cook the scallop, pour all the remaining dressing, no heat.
14. Give the dressing a good mix and discard in a small bowl.
15. Put one scallop per spoon.
16. On each scallop, put half a teaspoon of the diced pear.
17. With your warm dressing, drizzle some on top of the pear.
18. Finish with some Shiso cress, place the spoon on a serving tray and serve as soon as possible.

POTATO FRITTER AND ANCHOVIES

YIELD: 20 PIECES

POTATO FRITTER AND ANCHOVIES

YIELD: 20 PIECES

INGREDIENTS

- 100grs Spanish White Anchovies (Boquerones)
- 2 large desiree potato

Fritter mix
- 230 grs full milk
- 115 grs unsalted butter
- 150 grs plain Flour
- 4x eggs
- 2 tablespoon of chopped chives
- 2 pinch table salt
- a pinch of ground nutmeg

COOKING STEPS

1. Place the 2 potato in a pot covered with water and boil until soft.
2. When cooked, peel the potato and discard the skin.
3. Put the potato in a bowl and mash slightly with a fork, set aside.

Fritter mix

1. Place salt, nutmeg, milk and butter in a saucepan, heat over medium heat, stirring occasionally.
2. When the water is starting to boil (butter should be melted at this point), add the flour in one go.
3. Put the saucepan away from the heat and vigorously mix the flour in.
4. When the flour has absorbed the water and it's forming a dough, return the pan to the stove.
5. Transfer the dough to a bowl, and let it cool down slightly for a few minutes.
6. Mix the dough while adding the eggs one at a time, mixing well after each addition.
7. After the eggs, finish by adding the chopped chives and the mashed potato.
8. This fritter mix can be kept in a container, in the fridge to be use for the next day.

POTATO FRITTER AND ANCHOVIES

YIELD: 20 PIECES

PLATING UP

1. Take the fritter mix out from the fridge.
2. Preheat the fryer to 200c.
3. When the oil is at temperature, drop half a spoonful of dough in the oil.
4. Drop 20 portions of dough in the oil altogether.
5. When the fritters are nice and golden crispy, take them out and place on a paper towel.
6. Take 20 wooden skewers and skewer up white anchovies on each of them.
7. Stick one skewer in each fritter.
8. Place all the skewers on a tray and serve.

SMOKED SALMON AND HERB WAFFLE
YIELD: 20 PIECES

INGREDIENTS

Waffle
- 500grs plain flour
- 250grs butter
- 6x eggs
- ½ l full milk
- 20grs sugar
- 1 teaspoon baking powder
- 2 pinch of table salt

Garnish
- Heads of Chervil
- 100grs smoked salmon
- 20grs chopped Chervil
- 50grs Sour Cream
- 1 tablespoon of Horseradish cream (relish)

SMOKED SALMON AND HERB WAFFLE

YIELD: 20 PIECES

COOKING STEPS

Waffle

1. Separate the yolks from the white and measure all other ingredients.
2. Pick and wash all Chervil.
3. Keep 20 of the nicest heads of Chervil for garnish and chop all the remaining.
4. In a large mixing bowl, put the egg yolks, milk and melted butter.
5. Mix well and add the flour, sugar and baking powder.
6. Gently mix together, make sure you don't have any lumps.
7. Place all egg white in a bowl, add the salt.
8. Whisk them until they become white and fluffy, they should stick to the whisk (you can use a hand mixer).
9. Add the whipped meringue to the first flour mix 2 times.
10. Finish by adding the chopped Chervil.
11. You can keep this waffle mix in the fridge for a couple hours, but it is better to use it on the same day as serving.

Garnish

1. Take a slice of smoked salmon and cut small pieces about 3 cm squares.
2. Fold them in halves or roll them up and keep them on a plate in the fridge.
3. For the cream, mix the sour cream with the horseradish and place in a piping bag.

SMOKED SALMON AND HERB WAFFLE

YIELD: 20 PIECES

PLATING UP

1. Turn the waffle machine on and take the waffle mix out from the fridge.
2. When the waffle machine is at temperature, pour a large portion of waffle mix on the plate.
3. It should take less than 5 minutes, when the waffle is nice, golden brown and crispy, take it out from the waffle machine.
4. Repeat the same operation until you have used all waffle mix.
5. Then, cut the waffles in small squares, about 3 cm.
6. On each square, place a piece of the folded smoked salmon.
7. Pipe a little dot of sour cream on top of the salmon.
8. Put a small piece of nice Chervil and serve.

TUNA, AVOCADO AND SALMON CAVIAR

YIELD: 20 PIECES

TUNA, AVOCADO AND SALMON CAVIAR

YIELD: 20 PIECES

INGREDIENTS

- 500grs of Tuna loin
- 2 lime
- 1 tablespoon fish sauce
- 1 tablespoon soy sauce
- 1 tablespoon sesame oil
- 2 tablespoon pickled ginger
- 20 grs chopped chives
- 50grs chopped eschallots
- 4 large ripe Hass avocado
- 2 tablespoon EVOO
- 100grs Salmon Roe

COOKING STEPS

1. Peel and wash all eschallots and chives.
2. Chop the chives and ginger, dice the eschallots.
3. Peel all avocado and cut in small dices.
4. Add the EVOO, mix and set aside.
5. In a small bowl, mix the fish sauce, soy, sesame, the zest and juice of the limes, set this sauce aside.
6. Dice the Tuna fish around 5 mm thick.
7. n a large mixing bowl, add the tuna, eschallots and chives.
8. You can keep all the above sliced in covered containers in the fridge.

PLATING UP

1. Take all cut components out from the fridge.
2. Pour all the sauce over the tuna and gently mix thru.
3. Check the tuna seasoning.
4. Place all your small containers or jars on a large tray.
5. Fill them all up with the Tuna/Sauce mix, halfway up the containers.
6. Take the diced avocado and fill up the other half of the containers with it.
7. Finish by placing some Salmon Roe on the avocado, to cover half.
8. Place a small fork in it, or serve on the side.
9. Serve all on a serving platter.

MEAT

CHICKEN ROULADE AND JERUSALEM ARTICHOKE PUREE

YIELD: 18-20 PIECES

CHICKEN ROULADE AND JERUSALEM ARTICHOKE PUREE

YIELD: 18-20 PIECES

INGREDIENTS

- *59x Chicken thigh, deboned, no skin*
- *15x Basil leaves*
- *salt and pepper to taste*

Puree
- *200grs peeled Jerusalem Artichoke*
- *50grs cold diced Butter*
- *100ml full Milk*
- *Salt and pepper to taste*

Garnish
- *1 punnet baby basil*
- *30 grs corn kernels*
- *1 tablespoon of salted butter*

COOKING STEPS

1. Place a medium size pot full of water on high heat.
2. Place the chicken between 2 sheets of baking paper.
3. With a rolling pin, tap the top of the chicken to even the thickness.
4. Take some cling wrap and place 2 sheets on the bench, one on top of each other.
5. Put the "flattened" chicken on the cling wrap, one thigh next to each other, horizontally.
6. Season the chicken with salt and pepper.
7. In the middle of the chicken, place a line of basil leaves horizontally.
8. Roll the cling wrap up from the bottom to top.
9. Try to roll it as tight as possible, so it looks like a sausage.
10. Tigh-up each side of the rolled chicken.
11. Repeat the same operation with the rest of the chicken thigh.
12. When the water is boiling, turn the heat off.
13. Drop all the chicken rolls in the hot water.
14. Leave them in the pot for about 6-8 min.
15. Take the rolls out from the water and let them rest on a plate for another 10 minutes.
16. Place all rolls in the fridge for one night.

CHICKEN ROULADE AND JERUSALEM ARTICHOKE PUREE

YIELD: 18-20 PIECES

COOKING STEPS

Puree

1. Cut all the Jerusalem Artichoke in half.
2. In a medium saucepan, place all Artichoke, milk, salt and pepper.
3. Keep it on medium heat with a lid until it boils.
4. When the milk boils, take the lid off.
5. Turn the heat on low and keep boiling until almost no more liquid in the pan.
6. Check Jerusalem Artichoke, after 10 minutes it should be cooked thru.
7. Put all Artichoke in the blender, with the cold diced butter and seasoning.
8. Blend for 30 second until the puree is nice and smooth.
9. Discard in a plastic container, let it cool down for 10 minutes and store in the fridge.

CHICKEN ROULADE AND JERUSALEM ARTICHOKE PUREE

YIELD: 18-20 PIECES

PLATING UP

1. Place a medium size pot full of water on high heat with 2 pinch of salt.
2. Take the chicken and puree out from the fridge.
3. In a small saucepan melt the butter and add the corn kernel.
4. Cook the corn for about 2 minutes and set aside.
5. The puree can be reheated in the microwave for about 1 minutes.
6. When the puree is hot, give it a good mix to prevent the puree of splitting.
7. As soon as the water is boiling, place the chicken logs in the water, turn off the heat and cover it.
8. Leave the logs for about 8-10 minutes until they warm in the center.
9. Take the logs out from the water and dry them.
10. Remove the cling wrap.
11. Trim all edges from each log.
12. Slice each log into 6.
13. Put one piece per chinese spoon or little serving cups.
14. Place a small dollop of puree on top of the chicken.
15. Sprinkle a couple corn kernels.
16. Finish with a tip of baby basil.
17. Serve warm with a little tea fork.

CHORIZO ARANCINI, PIQUILLO SAUCE

YIELD: 15-20 PIECES

CHORIZO ARANCINI, PIQUILLO SAUCE

YIELD: 15-20 PIECES

INGREDIENTS

Risotto
- 500grs Risotto Rice
- 50grs unsalted butter
- 200grs diced Chorizo Sausage
- 1 tablespoon smoked paprika
- 10grs shallots peeled & finely diced
- 2 garlic clove finelychopped
- 2 tablespoons white wine
- 1.5 litres vegetable stock
- 100grs grated Parmesan cheese
- 200grs Creme Fraiche

Crumbing
- 5 whole eggs
- 100grs full milk
- 100grs Plain flour
- 100grs Japanese breadcrumbs

Sauce
- 200 grs whole egg Mayonnaise
- 100grs Piquillo Peppers (Charred Capsicum in a Jar)
- 1 tablespoon of Sherry Vinegar (Xeres Vinegar)
- a pinch of salt

COOKING STEPS

Risotto
1. Sauté off the shallots & garlic until soft.
2. Add the butter, rice and diced Chorizo.
3. Cook every off on medium heat
4. the Chorizo will release its beautiful oils and flavours into the rice, mix all to coat the rice.
5. Add the white wine, paprika and slowly add half of the stock, stirring all the time.
6. After almost all liquid has evaporated, add the other half of the stock.
7. Keep stirring until tender.
8. Remove from the stove.
9. Add the parmesan cheese and crème fraiche.
10. Mix gently until creamy.
11. Season to taste.
12. Take out into a clean tray & chill.

CHORIZO ARANCINI, PIQUILLO SAUCE

YIELD: 15-20 PIECES

COOKING STEPS

Crumbing

1. Once fully chilled roll into balls first around 30 to 40 grs each.
2. Then roll them in your palm, to give them a shape of small logs.
3. Place them all in the freezer for 5 minutes so they are harder and easier to crumb.
4. Roll in plain flour, dip in egg and milk mix.
5. Roll in Japanese breadcrumbs until evenly coated and nice shape.
6. Repeat the operation until no more risotto is left.
7. Keep all risotto in the fridge. (they can be kept in the freezer, just make sure to use sealed bags or container to prevent freezer burns)

Sauce

1. In a blender put all ingredients.
2. Blend quickly for 30 seconds.
3. Set in the fridge for at least 6 hours.

CHORIZO ARANCINI, PIQUILLO SAUCE

YIELD: 15-20 PIECES

PLATING UP

1. Preheat the fryer to 180c.
2. Take out the sauce and Arancinis out from the fridge. (if your Arancinins are frozen, place the Arancini in the fridge for at least 3 hours to defrost)
3. Deep fry about 10 Arancini for about 6-8 minutes.
4. When golden brown, check the temperature in the center to make sure they are hot.
5. Serve on the platter with some dots of capsicum sauce.

DUCK AND PEACH SKEWERS
YIELD: 18-20 PIECES

DUCK AND PEACH SKEWERS

YIELD: 18-20 PIECES

INGREDIENTS

Garnish
- 2 duck breast
- 2 large yellow peaches
- salt and pepper to season
- olive oil
- 1 bunch baby sorrel

Chimichurri
- 2 cloves garlic
- ½ bunch of fresh coriander
- ½ bunch of fresh continental parsley
- 1 red long chilli
- ½ cup orange juice
- 3 tablespoons red wine vinegar
- 8 tablespoons EVOO
- ½ teaspoon Xantana Powder

COOKING STEPS

Chimichurri

1. Peel the garlic and wash all herbs
2. In a blender put the garlic, chilli, herbs, orange juice, vinegar and oil.
3. Blend until the salsa is very smooth and free of chunks
4. Add the Xantana powder and blend for another 20 second
5. Check the consistency, add water if too thick or more Xantana if too thin
6. Keep in the fridge for at least 30 minutes, keep in mind the Xantana will make it slightly thicker once cold.

DUCK AND PEACH SKEWERS

YIELD: 18-20 PIECES

COOKING STEPS

Garnish

1. Place a non stick pan on high heat.
2. Season the duck breast on both sides.
3. Place the breast directly in the non stick pan, skin side down.
4. No need oil, the skin will render a lot of fat already.
5. As the pan heats up it will slowly render the fat.
6. When the pan is really, move the breast around so they do not stick and burn.
7. Reduce the heat to medium low, the goal is to render the fat as slow as possible to end up with a very thin and crispy skin layer.
8. It should take around 10 to 12 minute to end up with crispy skin.
9. Flip both breasts over and cook the other side for another 5 minutes.
10. Turn the heat off, take the breast out from the pan.
11. Place the breast on aluminum foil and wrap them.
12. Let the breast rest for 8 minutes, they will become very juicy and evenly cooked.

For the peach

1. Heat up the grill, as hot as possible.
2. Cut the Peaches in half.
3. Brush them with the olive oil and salt, pepper
4. Place the Peaches on the grill skin side up.
5. Very quickly make the grill mark, it should take only 1-2 minute.
6. Place them straight away in a container in the fridge to cool down.

DUCK AND PEACH SKEWERS

YIELD: 18-20 PIECES

PLATING UP

1. Take the duck, peach and sauce out from the fridge.
2. Cut the duck breast in small equal pieces, you should be able to have 18 to 20 small slices.
3. Cut each half peach into cubes, try to achieve the same size as the duck pieces.
4. On the skewers, start with a piece of peach first and then a piece of duck.
5. On a serving tray or platter, drizzle the Chimichurri.
6. Place each skewer on a serving tray.
7. Finish with a couple tips of baby sorrel.

LAMB CHOP WITH CHIMICHURRI

YIELD: 20 PIECES

INGREDIENTS

Garnish
- 20x Lamb chop trimmed and frenched
- 6 breakfast radishes
- 100grs shaved parmesan
- 50grs vegetable oil
- salt and pepper to season

Chimichurri
- 2 cloves garlic
- ½ bunch of fresh coriander
- ½ bunch of fresh continental parsley
- 1 red long chilli
- ½ cup orange juice
- 3 tablespoons red wine vinegar
- 8 tablespoons EVOO
- ½ teaspoon Xantana Powder

LAMB CHOP WITH CHIMICHURRI

YIELD: 20 PIECES

COOKING STEPS

Chimichurri

1. Peel the garlic and wash all herbs.
2. In a blender put the garlic, chilli, herbs, orange juice, vinegar and oil.
3. Blend until the salsa is very smooth and free of chunks
4. Add the Xantana powder and blend for another 20 second
5. Check the consistency, add water if too thick or more Xantana if too thin.
6. Keep in the fridge for at least 30 minutes, keep in mind the Xantana will make it slightly thicker once cold.

Garnish

1. Wash all radishes and slice them with a Japanese mandolin.
2. Slice them as thin as possible and rinse them with ice cold water.

PLATING UP

1. Leave the Lamb outside at room temperature.
2. Heat up the grill, until it starts to slightly be smoking.
3. Put some oil on the Lamb and season with salt and pepper.
4. Grill the Lamb chop on each side.
5. Make nice grill marks, 4-5 minutes per side.
6. When ready, place the Lamb chop on a plate on the side, to rest.
7. Resting, will allow the meat to become very juicy and evenly cooked.
8. On your serving platter drizzle some Chimichurri.
9. After 5 minutes rest, place each Lamb chop on this platter.
10. Place a dollop of Chimichurri on each chop.
11. Add some sliced radishes and sprinkle Parmesan cheese.
12. Serve immediately.

MINI PERI PERI CHICKEN BURGER
YIELD: 20 PIECES

MINI PERI PERI CHICKEN BURGER

YIELD: 20 PIECES

INGREDIENTS

Peri peri
- 5 chicken thigh deboned, skin off
- 5 cloves of garlic
- 1 large knob of ginger
- 5 large red chilli
- 2 bird eye chilli
- 1 tablespoon soy sauce
- 2 lemon

Garnish
- 20 small black brioche sliders
- 20 sprig of watercress
- 1 tablespoon of vegetable oil

Aioli
- 150grs whole egg mayonnaise
- 5 cloves of garlic
- 2 tablespoon of EVOO
- a pinch of salt

COOKING STEPS

Peri peri
1. In a blender, put the peeled garlic, both chilli, soy, peeled ginger and the zest and juice from the lemon.
2. Blend all until smooth.
3. Cut each chicken thigh into 4 pieces as equal in size as possible.
4. Place all chicken in a large container, completely flat.
5. Cover the chicken with the blended peri peri.
6. Mix all so the chicken is completely covered with the peri peri.
7. Leave the chicken in the fridge for one night.

Garnish
1. Wash all watercress.
2. Rinse and pick the nicessest heads.
3. Keep on wet paper in a container.

MINI PERI PERI CHICKEN BURGER

YIELD: 20 PIECES

COOKING STEPS

Aioli

1. In a blender place the EVOO, peeled garlic and salt.
2. Blend until smooth.
3. Then add the mayonnaise.
4. Blend all, one pulse at the time.
5. You want the aioli to be smooth with no chucks.
6. Keep the aioli covered in the fridge.

PLATING UP

1. Place a non-stick pan on high heat.
2. Add the oil in the pan.
3. Pan fry all chicken, 2-3 minute on each side.
4. When the chicken is ready place it aside on a plate.
5. Cut your brioche in half.
6. Add a teaspoon on each bottom brioche.
7. Place a piece of cooked chicken on top of the aioli.
8. Add a top of watercress and cover with the top of brioche

PORK AND PISTACHIO RILLETTES

YIELD: 20-25 PIECES

INGREDIENTS

- 5 1kg deboned pork neck
- 100grs white wine
- 2 bayleaf
- 4 cloves
- 2 brown onions
- 100grs sliced button mushroom
- 400grs water
- 1 sprig of rosemary
- 3 tablespoon Dijon mustard
- 100grs baby capers
- 100grs continental parsley
- 2 tablespoon ground pistachio
- 2 tablespoon chopped dried cranberry
- 2 red onion
- salt and pepper to taste

Garnish
- 100grs toasted Pistachio
- 100grs panko crumbs
- 1 tablespoon onion powder
- 1 teaspoon paprika powder

PORK AND PISTACHIO RILLETTES

YIELD: 20-25 PIECES

COOKING STEPS

1. Preheat the oven to 140c.
2. Cut the pork in 4 pieces.
3. Slice the onion and mushrooms.
4. In a deep baking tray or cast-iron pot, place the pork, onions, mushrooms, white wine, cloves, bay leaves, rosemary and water.
5. Cover with the lid or aluminum foil.
6. Place in the oven and bake for 3 hours.
7. Take the dish out from the oven, the pork should be very soft and should be breaking apart easily.
8. Remove the pork meat and keep it aside.
9. Place all leftover liquid and garnish on a medium pot and reduce on high heat.
10. While the liquid is reducing, break down all pork meat.
11. Flake the pork in a large mixing bowl.
12. Chop the capers, parsley and red onions, add it to the flaked pork.
13. Add the mustard and seasoning.
14. The liquid should be slightly thicker now.
15. When the liquid is reduced by ⅔, pass it through a strainer.
16. All garnish can be discarded.
17. The liquid is to be kept.
18. Pour the liquid in the large bowl with the pork, start only ⅓ of it.
19. Give it a good mix and add another ⅔ of the liquid.
20. Add the chopped pistachio and cranberry.
21. At this point mix again and taste if you need more salt or pepper.
22. It is up to you if you need to add more liquid or not.
23. Do you want it more wet or you like it dry.
24. For this recipe you need the rillette to be moist but yet hold a ball shape and not turning into a "pancake".
25. When you are happy with the taste and texture, you can choose the shape you prefer.
26. Small balls or small "quenelles", for this recipe we going to do balls
27. start rolling the balls in your hand.
28. Around 30grs each ball, nice and tight.
29. Place each ball on baking paper on a plate.
30. Cover the bowls with cling wrap and keep in the fridge.

PORK AND PISTACHIO RILLETTES

YIELD: 20-25 PIECES

PLATING UP

1. In a bender, place the panko, toasted pistachio, onion powder and paprika.
2. Blend all and put in a large mixing bowl.
3. Take the balls out from the fridge and roll them in these blended crumbs.
4. Make sure they are nicely coated and place the pork rillette on a serving platter.
5. Decorate with some pistachio kernels and edible flowers.

PUFFED LAMB WITH PEA PUREE
YIELD: 20 PIECES

PUFFED LAMB WITH PEA PUREE

YIELD: 20 PIECES

INGREDIENTS

Pea puree
- 400grs frozen peas
- 10 large leaves of fresh mint
- 200 grs cold Unsalted Butter
- salt to taste

Puff
- 500g Lamb Mince
- 1 tablespoon olive oil
- 5 cloves of garlic
- 1 brown onion
- 1 tablespoon of smoked paprika
- 30grs toasted pine nuts
- 1 tablespoon tomato paste
- 50grs white wine
- 100grs frozen peas
- 4 sprigs fresh thyme
- salt and pepper to taste
- 1 whole egg
- 5 sheets puff pastry
- 3x Egg Yolk for Glazing

Garnish
- a couple heads of fresh mint

COOKING STEPS

Pea puree
1. Place a medium pot of water on high heat, with 4 pinch of salt in the water
2. Dice the butter and put it back in the fridge
3. When the water is boiling, drop all peas in the boiling water.
4. Cook of the peas for 5 minutes.
5. The peas need to be cooked, soft but still bright and green.
6. When the peas are ready, drop all mint leaves in the water with the mint.
7. Stir the peas and mint, and strain immediately.
8. Keep ⅓ of the liquid.
9. In a blender, add all cooked peas and mint.
10. On top put the cold diced butter and salt.
11. Blend with rapid pulse, until smooth.
12. You can add a little bit of the cooking water that you kept to help the blending process.
13. Be careful not to add too much water, the texture of the puree should be still thick and creamy.
14. When ready check the seasoning and discard in a container for the fridge.

PUFFED LAMB WITH PEA PUREE

YIELD: 20 PIECES

COOKING STEPS
Puff

1. Defrost your Puff pastry or keep in the fridge overnight to defrost.
2. Chop the garlic, dice the onion and toast the pine nuts.
3. In a large pan, roast the Lamb mince with oil and garlic.
4. Keep mixing the mince with a wooden spoon to break up the mince chunks.
5. After 4-5 minutes add the diced onions and frozen peas.
6. Cook off for another 2 minutes.
7. When the lamb starts having a nice color, add the wine, tomato paste, thyme, frozen peas, paprika and seasoning.
8. Reduce the heat to low, mix well and cook until no more liquid.
9. When the liquid is gone turn off the heat and discard the mix in a large bowl.
10. Remove the thyme sprig.
11. Let it cool down for 5 minutes.
12. Add the pine nuts and the egg, mix immediately and your filling is ready.
13. With a round cutter, cut 10 cm wide circles.
14. In each center put a tablespoon full of mix.
15. Fold the edges back to form small parcels.
16. Stick the edges together.
17. Flip them over so the edges are hidden underneath, face down on a baking tray (with baking paper of course)
18. With a brush, cover each puff with egg yolk.
19. At this point they can be baked straight away or frozen for later use.

PUFFED LAMB WITH PEA PUREE

YIELD: 20 PIECES

PLATING UP

1. Preheat the oven to 200c.
2. If the puffs are frozen, let them defrosted on the tray for 10 minutes before baking.
3. Put the tray in the oven and bake for around 15 to 20 minutes.
4. Reheat the pea puree in a microwave for 1 minute.
5. When they are ready, take them out from the oven and let them cool down for 2 minutes.
6. Mix the puree well and put some on your serving platter.
7. Place the puffs nicely on top of the puree.
8. Finish with some mint and serve.

SIRLOIN BEEF ON PRAWN CRACKERS
YIELD: 20 PIECES

SIRLOIN BEEF ON PRAWN CRACKERS

YIELD: 20 PIECES

INGREDIENTS

Sauce Skid
- 150grs whole egg mayonnaise
- 2 cloves of garlic
- 2 tablespoon of EVOO
- 1 juice of a lime
- 1 tablespoon skid ink

Garnish
- 500grs sirloin beef sliced 1.5 cm thick
- salt and pepper to taste
- 1 tablespoon veg oil
- 2 tablespoon EVOO
- 20x prawn chips
- 1 punnet of baby Sorrel

COOKING STEPS

Sauce skid

1. In a blender place the EVOO, peeled garlic, lime juice and skid ink.
2. Blend until smooth.
3. Then add the mayonnaise.
4. Blend all, one pulse at the time.
5. You want the sauce to be smooth with no chucks.
6. Keep the sauce covered in the fridge.

SIRLOIN BEEF ON PRAWN CRACKERS

YIELD: 20 PIECES

COOKING STEPS

Garnish

1. Put a non stick pan on high heat.
2. Season the sirloin on both sides with salt and pepper.
3. When the pan is starting to slightly smoke, add the veg oil.
4. Straight away you can add the sirloin and color both sides.
5. Be careful as the pan is very hot, not to burn yourself.
6. You need the pan to be so hot to give a really nice crust and color to the meat.
7. It should drake you only 1-2 minute each side, then put the meat on a plate and let it rest for 10 minutes.
8. Preheat the fry to 300c.
9. Resting, will allow the meat to become very juicy and evenly cooked.
10. Then, on a cutting board, cut the meat around 2.5 cm square.
11. When the fryer oil is at temperature, drop the prawn crackers in it.
12. If the oil is hot enough they should puff straight away.
13. Stir them around in the oil so they puff evenly for 1 minute.
14. Take them out from the oil and place on absorbing kitchen paper.
15. Season straight away with salt.

SIRLOIN BEEF ON PRAWN CRACKERS

YIELD: 20 PIECES

PLATING UP

1. Have your serving tray ready, I find it easier to use crumbed up baking paper or new agency paper to place on the platter.
2. So when you place the prawn crackers on top they will all stand up the same way.
3. Place all your puff crackers on the paper.
4. Drizzle the EVOO on the beef and slightly glaze all squares so they become shiny.
5. In each cracker place a piece of beef.
6. Place a dollop of squid ink sauce on top of the beef.
7. Finish with some baby sorrel and serve.

WAGYU AND MANDARINS CIGARS
YIELD: 20 PIECES

WAGYU AND MANDARINS CIGARS

YIELD: 20 PIECES

INGREDIENTS

- *200grs minced Wagyu Beef*
- *4 mandarins*
- *1 tablespoon chopped coriander*
- *1 whole egg*
- *2 pinch of salt*
- *50 grs bread crumb*
- *1 packet brick pastry*
- *2 whole eggs for egg wash*

Sauce yogurt
- *150grs Coconut Yogurt*
- *1 teaspoon smoked paprika*
- *4x chopped Garlic*
- *salt to season*
- *1 tablespoon chopped coriander*

COOKING STEPS

1. In a large mixing bowl, put the wagyu, salt, zest of mandarins, coriander, egg and bread crumbs.
2. Mix all.
3. Place a small amount of mix in a pastry bag with a small pastry nozzle.
4. On the bench, place down the brick pastry.
5. cut them all in half.
6. Pipe one strip of Mix from one end to the other on each half brick pastry.
7. Leave 2 cm on each side.
8. Brush some egg wash on the brick pastry.
9. Roll up the brick pastry around the wagyu mix as tight as possible.
10. Place each cigar on a baking paper on a tray.
11. Keep in the fridge for 4 hours maximum, for later use you should freeze the cigars.

Sauce yogurt

1. In a medium mixing bowl, place all the ingredients and mix
2. taste and store in the fridge.

WAGYU AND MANDARINS CIGARS

YIELD: 20 PIECES

INGREDIENTS

1. Preheat the fryer to 180c.
2. Take out the sauce and cigars from the fridge.
3. When the oil is at temperature, drop the cigars in it.
4. The side will fry up and you will end up with a long thin cigar style, golden brown.
5. take the cigar out from the oil and dry on paper towel.
6. On the serving platter of your choice, place a small bowl with the yogurt sauce.
7. Stack up the cigars next to the sauce and serve straight away.

SWEET

BROWNIE SKEWERS
YIELD: 20 PIECES

BROWNIE SKEWERS
YIELD: 20 PIECES

INGREDIENTS

Chilli sauce
- 500grs Dark Chocolate (minimum 60%)
- 500grs unsalted Butter
- 350grs whole Eggs
- 400grs Sugar
- 210grs Plain Flour
- 1 pinch table Salt
- 5grs Baking powder
- 1 tablespoon Vanilla paste

Garnish
- 5 medium strawberry
- 1 punnet of Baby Mint cress

COOKING STEPS

Brownie
1. Pre-heat the oven to 150c.
2. Melted the chocolate and butter together in a bowl, you can use the microwave or on a bain-marie.
3. In a separate large bowl, whisk the eggs and sugar together.
4. Mix the egg and sugar for about 5 minutes until the mix is thicker and creamy.
5. Add all dry ingredients in the egg mix, the flour, baking powder, vanilla and salt.
6. Gently mix it all.
7. Then, add the chocolate/butter mix to the egg/dry ingredients.
8. Slowly mix until nice and smooth.
9. Put baking paper in your baking tray.
10. Pour your brownie mix on top of the baking paper.
11. Bake at 150 C for 25 minutes.
12. Let the brownie cool down for 30 minutes.
13. Place the brownie in the fridge.

BROWNIE SKEWERS
YIELD: 20 PIECES

PLATING UP

1. Take the brownie out from the fridge.
2. Cut small squares around 1,5 cm.
3. Wash and cut all strawberries.
4. Take the skewers and start by putting the cut strawberry.
5. Then stick them on the brownie squares.
6. Place all the skewers on a servicing tray or platter.
7. Finish with some baby Mint and serve.

CHOCOLATE GANACHE SPOONS
YIELD: 20 PIECES

CHOCOLATE GANACHE SPOONS

YIELD: 20 PIECES

INGREDIENTS

Ganache
- 260 grs pure cream
- 300 grs dark chocolate
- 40 grs maple syrup
- 50 grs butter
- 1 pinch salt

Garnish
- 100 grs speculoos biscuit
- 1 punnet edible violet flowers

COOKING STEPS

Ganache
1. Put the cream in a saucepan and bring it to a boil.
2. Meanwhile, chop the chocolate with a knife and place it in a separate bowl.
3. Add the cold diced butter and maple syrup into the chocolate.
4. Then pour the cream over it.
5. Mix with a spatula.
6. Dissolve the ingredients to obtain a smooth cream, make sure no more chocolate chunks are left.
7. Cover with cling wrap and let it cool.
8. Place the mixture in the fridge for at least one night until set.

Garnish
1. Take a large zip bag and put all speculoos inside.
2. Seal the bag and break all the biscuit by smashing the bag with a small pan.

CHOCOLATE GANACHE SPOONS

YIELD: 20 PIECES

PLATING UP

1. Take the ganache out from the fridge and place it in a large mixing bowl.
2. Whisk it until it becomes slightly thicker and creamy.
3. Place the ganache in a pastry piping bag with a large star nozzle.
4. Line up all serving spoons on a bench.
5. Pipe a little bit of ganache on each spoon.
6. Sprinkle some Speculoos crumbs on top of it.
7. Finish with a petal of edible violet and serve.

EATON MESS IN A GLASS
YIELD: 20 PIECES

EATON MESS IN A GLASS

YIELD: 20 PIECES

INGREDIENTS

Garnish
- 1 litre of pure cream
- 50grs sugar
- 2 vanilla bean
- 1 punnet baby kiwi
- 1 punnet fresh raspberry
- 200grs raspberry coulis
- 200grs white chocolate chips
- 10grs freeze dried mandarin
- 1 punnet baby lemon balm

Meringue
- 80grs caster sugar
- 40grs egg white

Elderflower Jelly
- 2 sheets gelatine
- 200grs Hot water
- 100grs Elderflower syrup

COOKING STEPS

Elderflower Jelly
1. Soak the gelatine in cold water for 30 min.
2. When the gelatine is re-hydrated, take them out from the water and press them to remove the excess water.
3. Place the gelatine in a bowl and pour the Hot water on top.
4. Add the Elderflower and mix until the gelatine is completely melted.
5. Pour the mix in a plastic container with a straight bottom, around 1 cm thick.
6. Put in the fridge and let it set for 3 hours.

EATON MESS IN A GLASS

YIELD: 20 PIECES

COOKING STEPS

Meringue

1. Place the egg white in the mixer bowl with a pinch of salt
2. Start whisking on full speed
3. After 10 seconds, you can add the sugar, gradually not all at once
4. Add half sugar first then the other half.
5. Keep whisking until the meringue is formed, with a "firm peak" texture
6. "firm peak" is when you remove the whisk from the meringue, and a stiff peak stands up firmly holding its shape.
7. Put the meringue in a pastry bag with a large star nozzle.
8. On a baking tray with baking paper, pipe tiny drops of meringue.
9. Place the baking tray in an oven at 80c.
10. Leave it overnight in the oven, it should take around 15 hours
11. You are just drying out the drops on a very low temperature, without giving any colour.
12. After 15 hours check if your drops are ready, they should be crispy and dry, without any moist part.
13. Store in an airtight container at room temperature.

Garnish

1. Wash and cut all fruits.
2. In a large bowl, put the cream, sugar and the inside of the vanilla beans.
3. Use a whisk and beat the cream until thick and fluffy.
4. This whisked cream is called a Chantilly.
5. Keep in the fridge until plating.

EATON MESS IN A GLASS
YIELD: 20 PIECES

PLATING UP

1. Have all your glasses or jars ready on a large tray.
2. Take the jelly and cut it around 1 cm square, keep in the fridge.
3. In the bottom of each glass, put a little bit of raspberry coulis.
4. Put the cream in a piping bag.
5. Cover the coulis with the chantilly, until ⅓ of the glass.
6. On the chantilly add a couple pieces of all different sliced fruits: kiwi, strawberry and raspberry.
7. Add 3 pieces of the cut jelly and a couple pieces of white chocolate chips.
8. If your chocolate chips are too big you can use a grater and grate the chocolate on top.
9. Sprinkle some freeze dry mandarin.
10. Finish with some head of lemon balm.
11. Serve with small teaspoons.

ICE CREAM SANDWICH
YIELD: 20 PIECES

INGREDIENTS

- 1kg of your favourite ice cream

Sponge
- 500grs Whole eggs
- 350 grs Caster sugar
- 375 grs Almond meal
- 100 grs plain Flour
- 75 grs unsalted butter melted
- 330 grs Egg whites
- 50 grs Caster sugar
- 1 tablespoon food colorant

ICE CREAM SANDWICH

YIELD: 20 PIECES

COOKING STEPS

Sponge
1. Sift all almond meal and flour.
2. Place whole eggs in Hobart bowl and start whisking
3. Add the sugar whisk the sabayon until ribbon stage
4. Gently fold in the almond meal, then flour and melted butter.
5. In a separate mixing bowl whisk the whites and add sugar till firm meringue.
6. Add the food colorant
7. Fold the meringue into sabayon.
8. Place baking paper on 4 large baking trays.
9. Divide mix into 4 and spread onto baking paper.
10. Spread till the whole tray is covered, no more than 3 mm thick.
11. Bake at 170 C for 6 minutes.
12. When cooked, remove from the oven and let them cool down.

Sandwich
1. Place a large mixing bowl in the fridge to make it very cold.
2. Take the ice cream out from the freezer and let it soften up for 20-30min at room temperature.
3. Place the ice cream in the cold large mixing bowl.
4. With a wooden spatula, mix the ice cream so it becomes light and creamy.
5. You want the ice cream to be easy to spread.
6. On a large tray, place one side of the sponge.
7. Cover the sponge with the ice cream, around 2 cm thick.
8. At this stage you could add potential garnishes, like sliced fruit or candies or chopped nuts. (optional)
9. Place another side of the sponge on top of the ice cream.
10. Place another tray on top of it.
11. Slightly press the top to make sure all is even and that the sponge are sticking together.
12. Place the whole tray in the freezer.
13. Repeat this operation until you have used all ice cream and sponges.
14. Leave all trays in the freezer for one night.

ICE CREAM SANDWICH

YIELD: 20 PIECES

PLATING UP

1. Take out the tray from the freezer.
2. Take a large Jug and fill it up with hot water.
3. Place a long chef knife in the hot water so it is easy to cut nic slices of ice cream.
4. Cut small ice cream sandwiches, 5cm square.
5. For each cut place the knife back in the Hot water and wipe the knife with a cloth.
6. When all the squares are cut you can place them on a serving tray.
7. Serve immediately or store in the freezer for later use.

MINI BASIL MADELEINES
YIELD: 20-25 PIECES

INGREDIENTS

- 4 eggs
- 1 teaspoon vanilla extract
- a pinch salt
- 90grs caster sugar
- 1 cup plain flour
- 70grs unsalted butter
- 2 limes
- 5 leaves of fresh basil

MINI BASIL MADELEINES
YIELD: 20-25 PIECES

COOKING STEPS

1. Melt butter and cook it for 2 minutes to give a very light brown colour.
2. Let the butter cool down at room temperature.
3. Chop the basil and add it to the mix.
4. In a Blender, add the eggs, vanilla, zest and juice from the limes, salt and Basil leaves.
5. Blend until really smooth.
6. Pour in a mixing bowl.
7. With a whisk mix in the sugar.
8. Gradually add the sugar until creamy and all sugar is dissolved.
9. Sift flour into egg mixture 1/3 at a time.
10. gently mix all together.
11. Add melted butter and mix.
12. You can keep this mix in a container, covered in the fridge.
13. But it is best to do the mix fresh, on the same day you like to bake and serve.

PLATING UP

1. Madeleines are best when you make the mix, bake and serve straight away.
2. Preheat oven to 200 degrees C.
3. In a pastry piping bag, put all the mix inside.
4. Pipe the mix in each mould, leave around 2 mm of the top of the mold, as the madeleines will rise slightly in the oven.
5. Bake 5 minutes, until the madeleines are golden brown.
6. Place them on your serving platter and serve Hot!

MASCARPONE IN A GLASS
YIELD: 20-25 PIECES

INGREDIENTS

Garnish
- 1kg Mascarpone Cream
- 700grs Pure Cream
- 100grs Icing Sugar
- 2 tablespoon Almond Essence
- 1 long black Coffee

Sponge
- 5x eggs
- 100grs sugar
- 110grs flour
- 1 pinch caster sugar

Coffee Jelly
- 2 sheets gelatine
- 200grs Hot water
- 100grs Kahlua

Garnish
- 4 shots of espresso coffee
- 2 tablespoon unsweetened cocoa powder

MASCARPONE IN A GLASS
YIELD: 20-25 PIECES

COOKING STEPS

Sponge
1. Preheat the oven to 180c.
2. In a large bowl, whisk the eggs with the sugar until thick and creamy.
3. Fold in the sifted flour.
4. Spread the mixture over a tray lined with baking paper and bake for about 6 to 8 minutes.
5. Remove from the oven when done.
6. Sprinkle it with caster sugar and allow it to cool.

Coffee jelly
1. Soak the gelatine in cold water for 30 min.
2. When the gelatine is re-hydrated, take them out from the water and press them to remove the exceedend water.
3. Place the gelatine in a bowl and pour the Hot water on top.
4. Add the Kahlua and mix until the gelatine is completely melted.
5. Pour the mix in a plastic container with a straight bottom, around 1 cm thick..
6. Put in the fridge and let it set for 3 hours.

Tiramisu cream
1. In a large mixing bowl, put all ingredients and whisk it all up.
2. The consistency will become close to a chantilly.
3. Place the cream in a piping bag with a large star nozzle.

MASCARPONE IN A GLASS
YIELD: 20-25 PIECES

PLATING UP

1. Place all little glasses or jars on a large tray.
2. Take the jelly and cut it around 1 cm square, keep in the fridge.
3. Cut the sponge around 2 cm square.
4. In each glass, place 3 pieces of sponges in the bottom.
5. Pour over the espresso coffee and let the sponge absorb it.
6. Pipe the tiramisu cream on top of the sponge.
7. Place 3 pieces of cut jelly on top.
8. Finish with cocoa powder.
9. It can be stored in the fridge for half a day or serve immediately.

SOURCING

This chapter is designed to help you find any products or equipment you might struggle to source. From platters to accessories, spices to products, I have put a list together of suppliers I used for providing me with all these items. I am not sponsored by them or making money in any way.
As I am based in Sydney and I try to use the best local and Australian options, all my suppliers are Sydney suppliers, but I am sure you can find similar options in any major cities around the globe.

PRODUCTS

Supermarket, Grocery
- Raz El Hanout / Goat's Curd/ Filo

Local Asian STORE (not online)
- Shizo Dressing (non oil Perilla)

Eustralis
- Yogurt Pots /Mini Tartlet /Duck Leg Confit /Plastic Pipettes/ Brick pastry/ Espelette pepper/ Metal spoon/ black brioche sliders

Paddy's Market
- Edible Flowers

Simon Johnson
- Truffle Paste (sauce)
- Xantana Powder

Two Providers
- Truffle Paste
- Shiso Vinegar
- Boquerones

Platters, serving ware, canape dishes, skewers and spoons
- Victoria's Basement
- Kitchen Capers
- Reward Hospitality
- Eustralis
- QCC Hospitality Suppliers

COPYRIGHT

Copyright © 2021 by Dominique Heitz
All Rights Reserved.

Created and written by Dominique Heitz.
Photography by Dominique Heitz and Bailey Wang.
Design and illustrations by Vivian Heitz.
Edited by Jimmy Siu-Bachelor of Education: Secondary Design and Teaching/ Hospitality.
Some pictures were edited with the Photoroom App and Prisma App.

1. Trademarks and brands are the property of their respective owners, no claim is made to them and no endorsement by them for this book or recipes are implied or claimed.

2. No part of this book may be reproduced or transmitted in any form or by any means, electronic or mechanical, including photocopying or by any information of brief quotations in a review.

3. The purpose of the book is to educate and entertain. The author or publisher does not guarantee that anyone following the techniques, suggestions, tips, ideas, or strategies will become successful.

4. Although the author and publisher have made every effort to ensure that the information in this book was correct at press time, the author and publisher do not assume and hereby disclaim any liability to any party for any loss, damage, or disruption caused by errors or omissions, whether such errors or omissions result from negligence, accident, or any other cause.

5. This book is not intended as a substitute for the medical advice of physicians. The reader should regularly consult a physician in matters relating to his/her health and particularly with respect to any symptoms that may require diagnosis or medical attention.

6. The author does not accept liability for any injury, loss or damage incurred by use of or reliance on the information contained in this book.

ONE MORE THING...

I would like to thank a couple people that helped me achieve this book.
I started this adventure without knowing if It was possible or even if I would like to do it.

I do not know yet if you enjoyed it, but one thing I know is that I had great fun throughout the process.
And I am looking forward to the next piece I will write.

I was lucky enough to have great support from my wife. My "pregnant wife" that is, who helped me design it and always gives me feedback with my progress. Of course, my parents, always supporting me and giving me the education and motivation to succeed as a Chef.

I started very young as you can see, in my "first" kitchen.
Also, I thank you, my audience for making it this far and hopefully you had as much pleasure reading it as I had writing it.

It is a small start and I am happy to tell you that it is only the beginning.
I plan to write many more. Many different topics, maybe with different languages but all related to food somehow...

If you did enjoy it and you would like to help me for any future book, please leave a review onthe platform where you purchased this book, Amazon, Facebook.
Also for even more yummy pictures, teaser of my next book, recipes and tasty news, follow me on my Instagram page, it is super easy, just point your camera on the QR on the right hand side.

DOMINIQUEHEITZ

HINT FOR NEXT BOOK

MY FAVORITE SWEETS COMING DIRECTLY
FROM THE CAPITAL OF CHRISTMAS?

www.ingramcontent.com/pod-product-compliance
Lightning Source LLC
LaVergne TN
LVHW061624070526
838199LV00070B/6569